NARCO COLOMBIANSNOW

mellow ben

Location EL Dorado International Airport, holding cells, time 13.13 pm

Well, Phil, here we go again, mate, this is it.'

Ok, ok Mr Sean, I wished we never came to this fecking place Colombia, five hours ago, we were sitting on the plane, going back home to Dundee, Scotland.

Now, Phil, I do not know what is going to happen now, This place has some of the hardest jails, in the world, there is no PlayStation here, or gyms and do not even think about watching television, this is going to be A real life changer, for the pair of us, no thanks to you Phil, I am sorry Mr Sean I will take all the blame, so you should Phil, you do not think I was going to take the responsibility, do you?

No, Mr Sean I told you before we came out to this place, to watch yourself, no but not you. You had to go and feck it up per usual, and you never stop to think of the consequence and look where we are, in a holding cell in Colombia and Phil do not kid yourself mate, there is no legal aid here, a lawyer isn't going to come walking through the door, and tell you and me everything is going to be just fine!

Now is he Phil?

Well, Mr Sean, I guess you're right.'

'Course I am right, Phil.

Money talks here, a person can buy anything with ready cash in jail here, look at the pair of us, and we do not have a pot to piss in, that is how bad things are going to be.

Yeah, you're right Mr Sean but we still have our families back home; Phil ok now, where are they going to get thousands of pounds, to bale the pair of us out of this mess, you have gotten us into? That is your problem, Phil, you never stop to think, that is all you have to do, is to stop and fecking think, it only takes a minute to think about the situation, and if you did that, we would be flying back home now, I cannot believe this is happening. You have been like this all through your life, mate.'

Remember four years ago, we had just walked out of the chip shop, after a few drinks in the town, walking down the side of the road were they were two policemen and just because you said one of them gave you a dirty look, you threw your mince pie in one of their faces? Yeah, Mr Sean, I remember that night, that was so fecking funny though to see the look in his eyes I think he wanted to kill me haha.'

Where did that get you? arrested, and a weekender in the cells?

Yes, Mr Sean, I do why? just listen to what am saying, Phil, ok, Will do Mr Sean.

And two months later, you were up in court, and the judge asked you do you plead guilty or not guilty, to police assault, and you said not guilty, yeah, course I do Mr Sean why?

And the Procurator Fiscal, read out the charge to the court, That on the 12th May 2015 at 9.45 pm, you did assault Police-Constable James P Mory care of Tayside Police, by throwing A projectile in the face of constable Mory. And you jumped up from the dock shouting, it wasnae a projectile - it was a pie.

That was the end of the trial, even before it started, you got fined £600 and £400 compensation. Mr Sean that was four years ago, why mention it now?

All I am saying is to stop and think before you say or do anything.

72 hours ago, I had the most beautiful girl I had ever seen. Maria, she likes me for who I am, I do not have the wealth she has, she knows that she had more money than the Queen of England and the rest of the royal family put together.

So, you and Maria, are you going to move into your one-bedroom flat back In Dundee then Mr Sean?

There you go, Phil, again you say the first thing that comes in to your head, I am telling you how I feel about her, and you're making a joke out of it. Will you ever see Maria again, Mr Sean?

Phil, worlds may change, galaxies may disintegrate, but a woman will always remain as a woman,

Yes, I am sure I will see Maria again, if it was not for Maria, talking up for the both of us, The DARK ONE would have let the werewolves ,vampires,(who are a breed of Ancient Aliens) ripped our body to pieces, not to mention all them fecking Sicarios. The way I see it, if we get five years, in the jail, we will do it standing our head after all that we have been through.

Yes, I know Mr Sean, but we will have to put our backs to the wall and go for it big boy.'

If we go into the jail acting like a couple of nutters going ahead with anyone, we will not make it Phil, it is the worst situation anybody can find themselves in, It is not like your fairy godmother going to pop up and say "click your heals three times" and be suddenly transported back home, now is it mate? It is the here and now Phil, the shit has hit the fan, how do you think Two Scottish guys, are going to fair in a Colombian prison?

I will tell you, Phil, it is going to be hard.

Yes, I know Mr Sean, but as you said before it is better than getting our body ripped to shreds by the werewolves and vampires, we will come out on top big boy.

Phil for the last time stop calling me big boy ok mate, Yeah, sure thing, Mr Sean.

"IT IS BETTER TO BE A CORPSE THAN A COWARD"

Mr Sean, what do you mean by that?'

You always have to watch your back in jail here, just until we get to know the in's and out's and get our feet under the table.'

What table Mr Sean?

Phil, are you stupid? Just press pause in that thick head of yours, and think about the last words I just said, you know Phil sometimes I think you have not got two oars in the water.

What do you mean by that, Mr Sean?

Forget about it, Phil, just fecking forget about it, mate, ok.

Yeah, Mr Sean will do, I am getting scared now, but we will get through it.'

Phil, you must stay focused, that is all you must do is to stay focused.

Ok, Mr Sean will do big boy.

Knock that on the head now, calling me big boy, and we are going into uncharted waters, the sharks are circling, and we do not have life vests. Four weeks ago, we were back home in Dundee Scotland, not care in the world, four weeks to the day you phone me, that when all this started with that fecking phone call...

Chapter 1

The present-day

In a land far, far away, *the mobile phone ringing,* 'where the hell is it? Under the bed'.

'Hello! Hey, Mr Sean', Phil here, "guess what?"

"You won the lottery?"

'No.' Phil.

'Well, what is It? I am still in my bed.'

Ok, I have won two tickets to see the Smoo, one of the biggest rock bands of all time in London, and an all-inclusive pass to the biggest nightclub in London where the Smoo is having a party to celebrate the last gig of their world tour! Everybody will be there, fellow rock stars, singers, actors, etc...., plus staying at the biggest 5-star hotel chains in the world, plus spending money as well, not bad, eh? Also, I got two pairs of anti-surveillance sunglasses, from 'Herbie big Baz.' *Now...I know you are wondering how he gets called Herbie big Baz, so I am going to tell you, Herbie was a 14-year-old football sensation, a "whiz kid" the highly sought after striker had already turned down offers from the French and German champions, and also the Scottish champions, fast-forward four years, as an 18-year-old he joined the Spanish giants "Barca" for a signing on fee of £4,000,000, his second game for the Catalonian giants, he was injured by a high kick to his groin, causing his testicles to swell up 12 times their average size. This, in turn, put an end to his professional football career. Hence the name "Herbie big Baz", he has got balls the size off elephants gum-sacks! He turned his hand and money to buying and selling counterfeit goods from the big warehouses in china - he sells some excellent quality merchandise but at a fraction of the designer labels.*

Mr Sean these sunglasses *you put them on and there are small mirrors in the inside of them so* you know if someone is following you. The DHSS maybe following you because you are "working under the radar," big boy and also I forgot to tell you, Mr Sean, *remember the Chinese couple, that lives around the corner from me - Mr & Mrs Wang, they have the Chinese takeaway? well they have just bought a dog, a cross between A springer spaniel and a Labrador.'*

Phil, I never knew they were vegetarians. 'Mr Sean,

Phil, it is a joke; think about it, mate.'

Oh, I see Mr Sean,

You do not get it, Phil, do you mate?

Nope, sorry, Mr Sean.'

I will tell you later, Phil.

Remember the old vintage USSR Soviet Russian Rare Portable TV ? black & white I picked up at the car boot sale about a month ago, well I got it working, all I did was took off the back and gave it a hoover all the tubes in the back of the tv were covered in dust.'

Phil, why are you wasting your time with an old black & white TV mate, everybody's got colour TV now?

Yeah, I know, I never got it to watch it mate, I will sell it on. I will place an advert on the internet. Somewhere, someone will be collecting them, I got it for £10 it is worth at least £100, mate. Later on in the afternoon, I am going up to give blood, at the blood transfusion unit at Ninewells hospital. I've have blessed with one of the rarest blood group types in the world - AB-negative, so I am doing my bit to help people that need AB-negative blood ok, big boy.

Here goes Phil again, I shrugged off his words as I thought to myself. (Mr Sean is a nickname from school that one of the teachers gave me, Mr Lee's and everybody calls me Mr Sean now, so I've changed my name from Sean to Mr Sean). Phil's, that's him, that's him on the phone, I've known him for 23 years, now I am 25 years old, I guess you can say all of my life, now, that's a long time, 'We stay in a place called. Well, you know the place, somewhere near you, the credit crunch has ripped the arse out of everything here, shops closing down, unemployment at an all-time high, and the cost of living goes up all the time, you know what I am saying.'

'So, what's happening today Mr Sean? *Phil said.*

Phil's voice suddenly brings me back to reality, and I replied. 'Well, I am going to play my saxophone for half an hour, and then, I've got to take Notch down to the vet's for his booster injection.' *Notch is my 7-month-old boxer dog, so it's time for his last injections. I named him Notch because I sponsor a white rhino in Kambara national park in Kenya when I was working but not anymore, I have no more money to do it anymore.* Then in the afternoon, I have to go down to the jobcentre, for some guy's coming to give the class of 20 people a talk. He is a motivational speaker. I'm telling you, you can get any job that you want, that you can do any job that you want to, there are thousands of jobs out there, you can be anybody you want to be. It is a load of shit, who is he trying to kid? there no jobs in Dundee except minimum wage jobs, bar work or cleaning tables at the local restaurant. If he thinks like that, well why is he not doing a better job than he is doing now? I bet when he was at school his dream job he wanted to do, was not to be a motivational speaker to a bunch of unemployed people, telling them that there are lots of jobs, when in fact there no fecking jobs. It is a lot of bullshit, Phil.'

I was on one of the course a few weeks back, Mr Sean, and a guy was telling the speaker, after he was at one of the class a few months back, that he got a part-time job, delivering newspapers, he got a job as a fecking paperboy! Not bad if you're a teenager, but this guy, Frank, I think that is his name, he is 38-year-old man.

4

All of the courses are a total waste of time. Phil, I will catch up with you later as I am doing something ok, mate.'

'Sure, mate chat later.

anyway, between you and me, I am joining an online dating site, and I'm not telling Phil that.

My profile will read as: *NAME; MR SEAN, AGE; 25 YEARS OLD, HEIGHT; 5'11" TALL...........*

HAIR COLOUR; LIGHT BROWN,

EYES; GREEN,

BODY TYPE; ATHLETIC,

HOBBIES; KEEP FIT, GOING TO GYM, CYCLING, LONG DISTANCE RUNNING,

EMPLOYMENT; UNEMPLOYED AT THE MOMENT BUT WORKING Sometimes AS MALE DANCER.

***

Phil and I have the same interest, and he is: 5'10", black hair, he is not a dancer.

Phil looks like an American Indian, his great-great-great grandad met and married an American Indian from the Cheyenne tribe a very long time ago, do not ask me how.

He looks like that Canadian actor, Keanu, you know the guy I am talking about, he has been in a lot of blockbuster films.

(Phil has a sixth sense, he has a psychometric abilities. This is a phenomenon where a person can sense the past with touch, or read the history of an object by touching it'. He cannot do it all the time, but I have seen it working. He once held a friends, great grandfathers old glove, and he was able to say who the owner was, where he came from, his wife's name and how many children the couple had, and the owner was wounded in the first world war, by a bullet in the right knee, and what job the person did, in his later years, and how the owner had passed away with a brain tumour and chronic heart disease. 75% of the information was correct, he very rarely has the ability to do it, but when he does Phil's spot on with most of the information) 'Are you ok, Mr Sean? You seem a bit distant, asked Phil.*

I raise my head. 'Yeah, well, I found Sue cheating on me last night.'

'You are joking, and you have only been seen her for a couple of weeks.'

'I know, I know Phil. What happened was this - it all started with our weekend away down to London to see her elder sister and her husband, Doreen, and Micky. On Friday we had book two seats on the bus, Dundee to London, it worked out about £14 each, the bus stopped at every major town in the UK; first Dundee, then Perth, Edinburgh, then on to Glasgow then it was down to England, Newcastle, onto Liverpool, Manchester, Birmingham, then last but no means least, London.'

Well, Mr Sean,' what is up with that?

Phil, we were on the bus for 16 hours, if we had paid an extra £10 each on the train it would only be 7 hours top mate. Doreen and Mickey meet myself and Sue, at the bus station. Sue was in the back of the car speaking with her sister, catching up with all the news from back home, so I am up front with mickey. He tells me, after we get to their house, and freshen up, they will take myself and sue clubbing. I said, sounds good to me mate! Their home was beautiful Phil, nice big house, lovely garden, 3 cars sitting on the driveway, both of them have very good jobs in computer IT. So, after we had a shower and quick bit to eat, then it was off to clubbing. We were driving for about 1 hour and 30 minutes, *I was thinking Mickey was lost,* then he turned left onto this massive driveway. At the end of the drive was a big mansion house with lots of cars parked outside it. "Knock, Knock, Knock" on the big door and then rang the bell a few times, and these three guys came to the door all dressed up in suits - white shirts and Kelly bows. Mickey took one of the guys to the side of the entrance, said something to him and passed his some money, and then we were in. Doreen did say to myself and Sue while in the car coming here - don't stare at people when we are in the club, I thought it was peculiar at first, but never thought anything about it.'

So why did she say that Mr Sean?

I am going to tell you, Phil, as we opened the other door, into the main room, the dance floor was full. Furthermore, everybody was naked; on the dance floor, most of the people there were exposed. Still, some people did have on their clothes. At first, I thought it was a swinger's club, a high-end swingers club, but then, I have seen people walking about with Gimp masks. They were wearing full-body rubber suits, and there were guys walking around on all fours, dressed up as dogs, and a girl is walking with them on leads! How some people get pleasure from doing that, it is beyond me, Phil.'

Well, Mr Sean, you know what they say, "do not knock it till you try it, big boy". It was the weirdest thing I have ever seen, and the girl's they were all dressed up in suspenders and fish-net stockings, *that was nice to see.* So, I was sitting looking amazed at these people, and this old lady, must have been about 80 plus, and dressed up in a little bo-peep outfit walk over to me, and put her hand down my trousers and said "I want you to eat me".

So, what did you say to her than Mr Sean?

I just looked her in the eyes and replied, sorry I am a vegetarian, and stood up and walked away. You never had to pay for any drinks. All of the upper-class people were there, getting drunk, snorting cocaine of the tables, the waitresses with their bunny outfits on getting groped by all the old perverts, and the females were groping the waiters as well, music blaring out.

I am not good with loud music as you know Phil.

Did you and Sue enjoy yourselves then, Mr Sean?

Not really Phil, I am not into all that stuff. At the end of the night, most of the people went outside and were diving into the big, heated pool. You could see the steam rising in the midnight air. Then it was back home, myself and Sue were arguing, so I booked a train journey back home the next day because I was not taking that bus ride home, total nightmare. So back home on Monday night. I was supposed to go to a psychic last night, Sue was staying in because she was not feeling well, but anyway, the psychic night got cancelled due to "unforeseen circumstances"'

'Well, Mr Sean, they must not be that good if they never saw it coming.'

'Hahaha, very funny Phil.'

I continue with my conversation. 'I am walking back to my house, and I see the bedroom lights on, so I go through the front door and hear music playing.'

'Well, what is up with that, Mr Sean?'

'It is the music we make love to.'

'Ah, I see, Mr Sean.'

Recalling the past events, I continued. 'And I hear someone saying, "you have got such a big tongue, big boy."' So, I burst into the bedroom, and there was sue, lying on the bed with no clothes on and Notch is licking cream off her "pussy."

'No fecking way, Mr Sean, what did you say?'

I screamed of course. ' what the feck are you doing", you do not know where that's been! I ran out the house, nobody sells doggie mouth wash, I had to go to the chemist and buy mouth rinse, poor Notchie-boy, he had blisters on his tongue.'

'Ha ha ha, Mr Sean, very funny.'

'I am only joking with you, Phil.'

'Yeah sure, Mr Sean, and here I am taking it in like a sponge. Have you split up with Sue, Mr Sean?'

'Yeah, Phil, she wanted me to stop male dancing, but I told her I could not stop it. I am finding it hard going as it is, living off £54 per week after I got paid, put money in the card-meter for electricity and gas and buying food, I am left with about £12 to last me all week, times are hard.'

Phil smiled. 'Don't I know it, Mr Sean, remember Mr Sean, we have got "Mercedes" engagement party on Friday.'

'Right, I forgot, she is getting engaged to that English guy, "Oliver," he is in the Royal Marines. or something like that.'

'Yeah Mr Sean, he is a Royal Marine commando, fuck, they do not like half blowing their own Trumpet. Have you seen their ad on the TV? Spiders crawling over the marines face as he stands like a statue? yeah some stupid young guy sitting and watching that on the TV will be thinking that is the 'dogs-bollocks', only because there are no jobs here for them to get. Hence, they get brain-washed into joining the British Army, which in turn changes them into killing machine to go to a foreign land to fight in someone else's war. Fighting for Queen and Country and then get discharged from the army with a medal for killing people in the name of Britain, and of every 10 of them are discharged, 4 will have a severe mental illness.'

I replied, 'Fuck that, I will stay here in Dundee, sorry Phil, that was me getting on my soap-box.'

'Mr Sean, everybody is entitled to their own opinion, not everybody will agree with it but hay-hoo, that is the life they choose big-boy. Mercedes, she has been a close friend since school, she has a lovely name, Mercedes and matching looks, she is a hot looking girl, long black hair always well-turned out, Ollie is a lucky man.'

'Phil, will Mercedes' brother be there?'

'He will be Mr Sean.'

'Remember, he ripped me off selling me that car.'

'Sure, do Mr Sean, you always go on about it. He's a con-man Mr Sean, and everybody knows that you never buy anything from him, and yeah, he is a drug dealer, a big-time one as well.'

'Phil, I never knew he would con me. I have known him for years and years. The car cost me £750, then I had to get the

Ford Escort insured, that was £450. It was only on the road for about two days until the traffic police stopped me for a bulb not working, then they told me a drug dealer once owned the car, and they will have to check over it- which was fine by me because I told them I do not take drugs and just because they never found any drugs, they even got in more police to check over the mechanics of the car and hit me with some bull shit. The car was not safe to be on the road, in all, there was about ten policemen/women at my car for about one hour.'

'and I bet in that time, the police were at the car, about two houses have been broken into, in the housing scheme! The police should get their priorities right and stop wasting time with little demeanours.' *Say, Sean, thinking to himself, Dundee police are like Poundland Colombo's.*

'at the end of the day, they took the car away and crushed it.'

'It is a sore one for you, Mr Sean.'

'So, Phil, I am going to have some fun with Mercs brother, Pete. That guy has never had a fulltime job in his life, all he does is deal drugs, he is so lazy he flushes bread down the toilet to feed the seagulls at the beach. I am going to teach that bastard once and for all, nobody rips off Mr Sean,

'Do you still have the Damagra? (damagra *is a genetic copy of the well-known male impotence pill for men who cannot get an erection*).'

'Yeah, Mr Sean, I have got about ten of them. Why?'

Looking at him straight in the eye, I responded. 'As I said, I am going to have some fun with Pete ok, I know he does not like butter or margarine on his sandwiches, so he is going to have some specially made up for him at the party. Now, this is where I need help, Kelly is coming to the party with me.'

'Mr Sean, you are a quick mover, you have just split up with Sue.'

'It is not like that Phil, although I wish - Kelly is a beautiful girl. She is a female dancer, works for the same company that I work for, and she's a lap-dancer as well, so she knows how to get a guy's attention. Pete has asked her out loads of times, but he always gets a knockback.'

'Here, Mr Sean, will Pete's girlfriend not be there? What is her name again?

'Liz (fatty) Ray?', (*she is that stupid girl, she got fired for a BLOW JOB*) 'No, she will not be there as she is working as a pole dancer, feck off.'

Mr Sean, she is well too fat to be a pole dancer, she weighs about 340 LB, she has got an ass the size of an Aberdeen Angus.

(Aberdeen Angus is a big fat cow) "Ladies and gentlemen, you *have to man to fuck up, or you will not make it to the end of this book.*"

'Yes, I know Phil, she is a telegraph-pole dancer, she was the first girl in Dundee to get an "asbo" from the council for climbing on the telegraph-poles because she is always breaking them.' *nodding his head, Phil looks back at me.* 'Good one, Mr Sean.'

She was that fat when she was at school, she sat beside everybody, she went on holiday sunbathing on the beach, with her bikini on, the Japanese whaling ship was firing harpoons at her.

'And Phil, her pal is coming as well, Sabrina? So, we can all go as partners.'

'Well done, Mr Sean, Sabrina's is a honey as well.'

'Yeah but remember, the girls are coming to play the part, it is not sexual in any way Phil.'

'Shit, I thought my luck was in Mr Sean.'

'Sure, Phil, you are dreaming.'

'She is always saying I look like that film actor "Keanu."'

'Well, Phil, if you do not try, you will not get, but the most you may get is a few dances.'

'That is all I need, Mr Sean.'

'Well, you will be on the first step, good luck, I will tell you something, Phil.'

Ok, Mr Sean go for it",

If you had the money "Keanu" has, and with your looks mate, you would have girls falling at your feet mate. Girls would be hitting on you all the time Phil, and no doubt some guys as well, Phil, I would be hitting on you myself mate.'

Mr Sean, you have never said that to me before, but not on the first date Mr Sean.'

Phil, for feck sake, it is a figure of speech; stop and think about it, mate.'

I ken Mr Sean I am just playing along with you mate, that is all.

***

FRIDAY NIGHT

Mercedes engagement.

Staring at the lovely looking ladies, I wave at them. 'Hello, Kelly, Sabrina, both of you are looking lovely as always. Are you all ready for some fun time?'

'Yes, Mr Sean, where is Phil? Is he not coming?' Sabrina asks.

'Yeah, he will be here in one moment, he is running late, here he is now.'

I notice Sabrina looking in the direction of Phil, who was almost running towards them. 'Come on Phil, we are all waiting for you.'

'Sorry, I had to look for the tablets. Mr Sean and ladies, you are all looking lovely tonight.'

Sabrina blushes. 'You brushed up not bad as well, Phil.'

Phil smiles and replies. 'Why, thank you, Sabrina.'

Sabrina is a lovely redhead, super-good lady with looks and an ass to die for, as do all the young girls that work with me.

Time has come. 'Right, this is the plan Kelly. Pete's going to ask you to have a dance with him. After the dance, he is going to buy you a few drinks; he will think he has scored with you. I need you to go over to the food table, and there will be a few plates with cling film on them with Pete's name.'

'How do you know that Mr Sean?'

'Well, because every party he's been at, he always has his food separated from the others, because he does not like butter or margarine.'

'Now, Kelly, this is where you come in, I need you to put two of these, "100mg Damagra tablets" into his sandwiches and make sure you hand him the one that's got the tablets in, they take about 20 minutes to work, but he has to be sexually aroused, so after he has eaten the sandwiches, get him up on the dance floor and start making some erotic dance moves on him, go back to the seats and start sitting on his lap and start doing a wee lap-dance on him, but be discreet about it. Afterwards, look over at me, and I will give you the nod for you to go to the toilet and leave the rest to me.'

'Ok, Kelly, you know what you have to do.'

'Yes, Mr Sean, I cannot wait to see the result.'

'Right, let us go to the party, guys.' *I said, deviously smiling.*

At the party, it is busy, there must be about 80 people.

Phil calmly gestures to a waiter at the party. 'Mercedes says she is expecting about 150 people to be here at the end of the night. Here, Mr Sean, there a bunch of guys waving at you over there at that table.'

'Yeah, Phil, that is the guys I worked with when I was a summer employee last year.'

'So why are they here, Mr Sean?'

I sip my drink. 'Because Mercedes works with them as well.'

My eye scans the room as I look in their direction, lost in my thoughts. Ronnie, "Scorpion" Paul, "Aggie" Stephen "the Bibster," Jim "Gossie the pussy," (he thinks he gets called gossie the pussy because he is a big hit with the girls). Then, there is Ian, "Arms" because he pumps iron, and Damon "Damo," Ron "Rocket Ron," and then, there is Steve, "Shanado," he works as a gravedigger. There is Stuart, "Stuart boy", then Owen, and finally, there is Alex, "Oh Eckie, what have you done."

Alex took every drug under the sun; about ten times, most of them are ok but like everywhere you work, these are always some assholes.

See the guy walking back from the bar with a tray full of drinks.' Sure, do Mr Sean why?

I am going to wave him over, wait till you hear his story about getting revenge. His name's Sean, here he comes now.' Hey Mr Sean, how are you doing mate, are you coming back working with the department again this year.

Hope so, I will have to wait until the jobs are advertised later, it should not be long now.'

Maybe a couple of weeks now, Mr Sean.

Sean are you going to tell Phil about the time when you were getting harassed by that supervisor Grant Smurnet?

Yeah sure, but will have to keep it short. Right Phil there is a supervisor in the work called Grant Smurnet, he is a total asshole, he thinks he is better than everybody else. If you tell him you were on holiday and staying in a 5-star hotel, he would say he stays in 6-star hotels when he is on holiday. He always has to be one better than everybody else. Nobody likes him, even other supervisors think he is a prick. He is always kissing his Freemason ring he wears. So, he started harassing me. Every day he would come down to my work place, first thing in the morning, last thing at night, all through the day, watching me, he would raise his voice, trying to get a reaction from me. He would have loved me to hit him in front of a witness, to get me paid off. So this was going on for about six weeks, but in that time I was writing everything down, and I had written a letter about him harassing me and I sent it to the Personel Department and to the councillors also who were in charge of the department, and the various god fathers of the council, in all I sent about ten letters. Anyway, to cut a long story short, I was on the football at the weekend taking in money for the pitches and changing rooms. The football got cancelled where I was, so I had to go up to Sorefield Pavilion. The bottom of Pavilion was the changing rooms and showers, while the top half was where the supervisors and manager were, so I tried the door, and it was left opened so I went up to the kitchen to make myself a cup of tea, and there it was Mr Sean.'

Anyway, there was what Sean?

Grant Smurnet, the cup had writing on it, *Grant no 1 Ranger supporter, in the world.*

Now bear in mind this guy harassed me for about two months, so I said feck you Smurnet. I was going to urinate in it, but was thinking most people rinse out their mugs with water especially if it's been lying around all weekend, so I stuck my two fingers up my asshole and rimmed them around the inside, and outside of the mug, I did this a good few times. A few days after that I was up at Sorefield at a meeting with other people, all the people had to walk past where the supervisors office desks were in the big room, to get to the meeting room, and Grant Smurnet was sitting at his desk looking lost. He knew someone did it, but he does not know it was me. It serves him right for picking on people, especially me, feck you, Grant. Right, Mr Sean, Phil, I will have to get back to the table. Enjoy yourself boys and have an excellent night ok.

Yeah, Sean, we will. Have a good time mate, catch up with you later on, - forgot to say, Sean where's your friend, Ozzi Mcpliers? He never goes to nights out, would you believe it Mr Sean Mcpliers reported me to the supervisor, saying I was talking about gay men, and that I was referring to him.'

After all the derogatory remarks he said about you Sean.

Yeah I know Mr Sean, you see he could not get the better of me, so he thought he would play the "I am a homosexual card," and get me into trouble at work, but I have nothing against gay people - I have nothing against anybody. So the chargehand *Ron,* came in to tell me that Ozzi Mcpliers has a letter written out and ready to go to the Human Resources, about me. So, Mr Sean, Mcpliers was wanting me to apologise to him for talking about gay people in his company when he is gay, where is the logic in that? I told Ron if he cannot take it do not give it out, and as for the letter stick it where the sun does not shine. Now, Mc pliers does not even look at me, he's a first-class belter. Anyway boys, good to see you all and you're looking well, take care men ok.

See you around Sean, take care.'

Here Mr Sean, that was a childish thing to do about reporting Sean was it not?

It sure was Phil, but hey, that is a workplace for you, some are right two face bastards. I have seen it with my own eyes, Phil. Moreover, about the cup of tea, that was a disgusting thing to do, I bet he does not make the tea for his workmates.

It sure was Phil, but that supervisor he was talking about is a first-class asshole mate, and you learn something new everyday Phil furthermore, what is that Mr Sean?

Never let Sean make you a cup of tea!

'Here Mr Sean, that is the guy from your work over there, the one you saw kissing his 12-year-old nephew on the lips.'

I nod with my head. 'Ozzi Mcpliers, no that is him, Sean was talking about, he is very s-t-r-a-n-g-e, he never talks to any of the women at work, he gives them a dirty look.'

'So, he is a misogynist?' *Phil asks.*

'Yeah Phil, you have knocked it on the head there mate, and he can be a right cheeky bastard. One of the guys he works with told me that Ozzi said to him if you went to a party and woke up the next day in bed with two guys and had a sore ass would you tell anyone, the guy's said, "No fecking way man!" and Ozzi said to him you, "fancy coming to a party"'

'Ha ha ha, is that just not workmates talking Mr Sean.'

'Phil, Ozzi had just met the guy two days before, and Mc pliers told him that he is the "number one cock fencing champion in Scotland."

What the feck is cock fencing is that like something in the homosexual Olympics?

Must be something like that mate, why are you thinking about going in for it?

'no, I am just curious that's all, he is defo a first-class homosexual then, is he Mr Sean?'

That Ozzi Mcpliers ex-boyfriend wrote on the public toilet walls, what is the difference between 7 black men and a joke? and under it he wrote, Ozzi cannot take a joke.

That is a nasty thing to say about the guy, but right enough, some of them can be very bitchy, Mr Sean.

Phil the world's is full of capital letters, people, *Capital letters people* explain yourself, Mr Sean?

These *capital letters, people* are LGBT *lesbians, homosexuals, bisexuals, and transgender people,* just like one big happy family, well not Phil.'

You are speaking with forked tongue mate?

Well, Phil, the *lesbians* are always bitching about what clothes the gay men are wearing, and the *gay men* are always bitching about how the *lesbians* are dressing, so the *lesbians* should not wear the clothes the gays are wearing and vice versa, but everyone likes the *bisexuals* Phil.'

And why is that Mr Sean?

Because the *bisexuals* will fuck any of them, they will even have sex with the *transgender people.'*

That is something I do not agree on Mr Sean, if you are born with a penis then you are a man, and if you are born with a vagina, then you are a woman. A man cannot be born into a woman's body, and a woman cannot be born into a man's body.'

How the hell do you work that one out, Phil?

Well that's just like a black man saying, he was born into a white body, and the guy says hello da're man, me be a white Rastafarian wearing Rastcap and smoking a big marijuana reefer, playing the calypso drums, at the Notting Hill Carnival or the Nayabinghi, with his white dreadlocks, singing "nae woman nae cry," or a white man born into a black man's body, acting like a white man, saying roger gangs away ginger, rather spiffing day, fancy some afternoon tea, that shit isn't never going to happen mate is it!

I know how *transgender people* get your back up Phil, remember our first-holiday Spain Gran Canaria, Our first night there, we went out clubbing, and you were looking at that African girl on the dance floor all night, then you plucked up enough courage to ask her to dance, and at the end of the night you went back to her apartment.'

For feck sake mate why did you bring that up, I never knew he/she was one of them, *transgender people.* You knew he was she but you never told me, Mr Sean. I was wondering why everybody was taking our photos and pointing at the pair of us on the dance floor, I thought it was because we were good dancers.'

Phil, you should have known it was a guy. Put it this way how many girls do you know has an Adam's apple? I will tell you Phil none, because female does not have an Adam apple. I sniffed him out like a Truffle pig mate, I went to the bar to get a few drinks, and you were away with him. I tried to phone you, but you'd had turned off your mobile phone mate.'

Anyway Mr Sean, I was shocked at first, but I said feck it I am on holiday, I never had sex with him I just Diddie fucked her, *it does not make me gay, it's just like the real thing mate.* And in the morning we had cheese on toast, as I was going to the door she grabbed me by the hips pulling myself towards him/her looking into my eyes saying I would like to see you again *Philippe,* I think you are a wonderful person, you were so kind to me when I told you I was born a man and had the operation to become a woman *(Katrina),* and you said it was such a lovely name, even though you had a good few beers that night, you were so kind and caring.

Did he kiss you then, Phil?

No Mr Sean, I just pushed him away and said, you know, Mr Sean is never going to let me live this down, you are fucking freak of nature and *"kicked him in the pussy."*

Phil, I think you are homophobic mate; from on now, I am going to call you Darth Gaydar.

No way, Mr Sean, I am not homophobic, that's just like saying gay men are pussyaphobic because they don't like pussy mate.

'Phil, we're in the 2020's mate the world's changing, everything goes now Phil, we are all *"Jack Thomson's bairns"*. Homosexuals are the norm now Phil - anyway, it's his life, he can do what he wants too, but it's all comeback and bites him in the ass now. One of the gardeners up in Hawk-son park was getting his tea-bags and other items stolen from his locker, so the guy big Tam, (he has got a voice like a fog-horn, you hear him before you see him), he is a sound guy; anyway, Tam set up a spy camera overlooking his locker, and when someone passes the locker it comes up on his I-phone and records automatically. He saw Ozzi Mcpliers performing a sexual act on one of the other gardeners, a guy named Ian Sleekier.'

"Did a sex act", Mr Sean?

'Feck sake, Phil use your imagination, he was sucking his c*ck like it had the antidote in it, so Tam put it on social media for everyone to see because like I said, Mcpliers can be real cheeky sometimes and calls Ozzi "secret sausage jockey". He is just getting his own back because, like most of them, they can be very bitchy like a woman scorned.'

'So, Mr Sean, do you think he is a nonce?' (*nonce is a slang word for a paedophile*) 'I do not know Phil, but how many 32-year-old men do you know that kisses 12 years old boys on the lips?'

'Yeah, I understand what you are saying, Mr Sean, so what does he look like then Mr Sean?'

'He is about 5'10" tall, stocky build, crew-cut hair, light brownish hair, and he wears these wire rim glasses, very well-spoken and he is well educated Phil. as well'

'So, Mr Sean, what is he doing working with you and all of them over there if he is well educated.'

'Very funny, Phil, what is the difference between a straight man and a bisexual Phil.'

Aye dinnae ken Mr Sean?

Eight pints and six vodkas.

The music was deafening, and I touch my ear with the palm of my hand to draw out the sound of the loud music.

'I do not see any of their girlfriends, and it must be a work night out after which they will go and watch the heavyweight boxing match down in the local bar tonight. Anyway, back to the plan.'

My glass cup was almost empty. 'Right, I will go up to the bar what is everybody drinking?'

Phil looks at me; I could tell he knows I plan to get more drinks.

'Just get cokes, and we will wait and see how the party goes.'

I stood up and replied to him. 'sure, no problem.'

So, I am up at the bar getting the coke and drinks, and someone calls out my name.

'Hey, Mr Sean, how are you doing? Still looking to buy a car?'

'Hahaha, very funny, Pete, just like the last one you sold me.'

'Are you going out with Kelly, Mr Sean?'

'No way man, I wish - she is just here with Sabrina because she is on a sort of date with Phil.'

'Lucky Phil, Mr Sean, so it would not bother you if I asked Kelly up on the dance floor.'

'Help yourself, Phil.'

'I will catch up with you after Mr Sean.'

'Yeah, Pete, you better believe it.'

'Here are your drinks girls - Pete took the bait. Kelly, he is going to ask you out for a dance, and he is looking over right now. Here he comes, Kelly, get ready.'

Kelly is up on the dance floor, doing all her moves, and Peter's loving it.

She had gone over to the food table now, and she did it, she has put the two tablets in Peter's sandwich. This is good, she is sitting on his lap feeding him the sandwich, it will take about 15 to 20 minutes to start to work. 15 minutes later, I nod in the direction of Pete.

'That is it Phil, it is working, he is touching his crotch, that is Kelly going to the ladies room, now for plan B.'

'What is the plan, B Mr Sean?'

'Just watch, I am going to get the mic of the DJ and say a few words about the happy couple.'

I walk up to the stage and pick up the mic. 'Ladies and gentlemen, can I have your attention, please?

I want to thank everybody for coming tonight for Mercedes and Oliver's engagement, and most of all, I would like to thank Mercedes brother, Pete, for putting on a lovely food spread and for buying everybody three rounds of drinks like a big thank you for everybody coming tonight.

At this point, Pete is sitting there with his red face, the tablets are now working.

I continue. 'Pete was telling me in the toilets that he is going to Thailand to look for a ladyboy to marry and bring back over here to Dundee with him. *At this point, everybody was looking at*

Pete. let us have a big round of applause for Pete, and Pete, let us have you up on the stage for a few words.'

I am now blowing him kisses and waving at him as he gets up, I said to him. 'Hey Pete, I never knew you liked me that much, is that a banana in your pocket or are you just happy to see me. I point to the erection in his trousers. Everybody was pointing and laughing at Pete with his hard-on. Peter just stormed out of the place. *That will teach him to rip me off, asshole, mission completed, job well done.'*

'Here, Mr Sean, that was a good one you got on Pete.'

'Yeah I know - he deserved it.'

'Mr Sean, you better get out of here, because he will be looking for a way to get his heavies down to take care of you.'

'Sure, I fear a bunch of guys that take steroids Phil, but for Mercedes, I will go as I do not want to upset Mercedes and Oliver's night.'

Later, at the gym, I wipe the sweat off the right side of my face using a towel I brought along from home. 'Right, that is me finished here, Phil, are you going down to the gym tomorrow, say about 2 pm?'

'Yes, Mr Sean cool, see you then.'

'Ok, I will see you there at about 2 pm ok, Phil.'

'Yeah sure, hope Frankie will be there to open the side door.' Asked Phil.

'He is always there.' Frankie is a really good mate, and he works the nightshift in the local bakery. He is always working out at the gym, keeps on telling me about all the girls he gets, and going on about how chiselled his body is, and how the girls like it. To tell you the truth, I've never seen him with a girl in my life, I think the last time he felt a pussy, it was around his neck. *(get it)* Frankie, you're typical poser, always under the sunbeds (he has even got a better tan than Mr Asif who works in the corner shop) bleach teeth, never a hair out of place, you all know the sort of guy I am talking about. It is all a show with Frankie; I think he feels Emasculated when I am in his presence.

Can you blame him?

After the gym work out, we went around to Phil's house, and he explained more about the prize he has won in the radio competition.

I grabbed a packet of biscuits Phil had sitting on the table in the living room where we are seated, and I looked up at Phil. 'Well Phil, that the best thing that's happened to you and me in a long time.'

'Yes, I know,' said Phil with a cheeky smirk on his face. '7 days and counting, cannot wait to get out of this place, even for few days, this is going to be a perfect break for the pair of us, and this night club is going to be full, with loads of gorgeous looking woman.'

'Phil, we have no chance with these women, we are two unemployed guys, who do not have any money.'

'Yeah yeah, yeah, Mr Sean, but nobody knows that we can be anything you want, antiquities dealers, businessmen, anything you want for one night.'

'Ye feck it, Phil, let's go for it. Wait a minute Phil, this Saturday, I am stripping at a gig (I work most weekends as a male stripper to get some extra money) 'That is ok, Mr Sean, we are not leaving till Tuesday.'

'Yeah sure, Phil.' 'I could not strip in front of people, it is not my scene Mr Sean, taking all my clothes off?'

'You do not take all your clothes off Phil; you keep your little fella covered when the girls have a drink on them, and the music is playing. It is an excellent atmosphere, plus I get a lot of girl's phone numbers and put them in my chicktionary, and better still, I get paid for it, what is more.'

'Do you always have to show off your body Mr Sean?'

'I do not work out at the gym, to keep my body covered up, do I, Phil! If you got it, flaunt it. Frankie thinks he has got a chiselled body, and he has not seen me with my top off.'

'Ok Mr Sean, I will phone you tomorrow after your gig, yeah cool, speak to you then, Phil.

***

My phone rings loudly, I reach out to pick up the call while thinking to myself how annoying my present ringtone is. I must change this ringtone to another one.

'Hullo.' 'Hey Mr Sean, Phil here, how did your gig go last night?'

'It was a total nightmare, Phil.'

'Well, tell me what happened!'

'So, I am at the gig all pumped up, oil is on my body, so the manager says, Mr Sean, you are on, so I walk out on to the stage and ….'

'And what Mr Sean?'

'It is all men, not a woman in the place, and even the bartenders were all males.'

Well, what is up with that, Mr Sean?

Earth calling Phil, come in Phil, think about it, it is all men that like the company of other men.

'Phil, are you going to stop laughing so I can tell you what happened.'

'Yeah, sorry, Mr Sean, but it is funny.'

'Not for me, it was not funny, anyway... I walk off the stage and my manager, Mr Shanley, you know the guy - he is always dressed in white, wears a Panama hat, runs all the strippers and the gentlemen's clubs in town, he looks like that guy Boss

Hogg of that early 80's TV program, the Dukes of Hazardous, or something like that, anyway he comes in with the guy that made the booking. They are complaining that I'm not going on the stage to perform, I told them, I don't strip in front of men, only females. Mr Shanley, my manager, says he is paying me double my pay for the night, and the guy that has booked me was sitting there crying. No way, Mr frankly, I am not going out there in front of all those men, taking my clothes off, that is it, final. He tells me "you will never work stripping in this town again Mr Sean" and I replied, "Quite frankly Mr Shanley, I do not give a fuck."'

'Never mind.' Phil said. 'You know what they say.'

'What is that Phil?'

A little bit of brownnn never let you downnnnn, "like to point out that I have nothing against gay people males or females".

'Yeah, Phil, it also says in the black book, "man shall not lie with man and woman shall not lie with a woman." Anyway, forget about it, Phil, will you see Jackie, your sister?'

Jackie is a lovely looking girl, blue eyes, blond hair, all the right bumps in all the right places, about 5"3 tall, 34 years young, she looks like 24, first-class honey Phil nods his head as if he is listening to music. 'Yes, she will be in soon.' 'Can you get some day passes for the sauna?'

I smile to myself and think of how wonderful Jackie has been to us. Jackie works at a beautician, a massage therapist in a 4-star hotel in town, and at times gives Phil and me day passes.

Jerking out of my thoughts. 'Jackie is always winking at me *(and you know what a guy thinks when a girl winks at them, right guys?),* but I have noticed, she winks at all the guys, especially the male customers at her work.'

Looking uncomfortable, Phil responds. 'I think it is just part of her body language, and she probably does not know she is doing it.'

'Yeah, right.'

I was lost in my thoughts again. Phil thinks the world of his sister; I have not told him, she has been with most of the men from the club, in the hotel, they call her the blow job queen of the sauna, she has swallowed more semen than the Bermuda triangle.

Phil, who is the guy that goes to the gym that wears the fluorescent t-shirt and has one of the legs of his shorts, rolled up his leg?'

Is that the guy that wears they big daft headphones?

That is him, Phil, he walks around the place as he owns it.

Yeah, Mr Sean, I know him, he used to be the lead singer in an indie rock band called the Blockers, I think. They are from Dundee, their debut album released in 2010. He believes he's a super rock star, like Bono, they only had the one album, and then split up after that. Jackie, my sister says, he thinks he is gods gift to women, all the girls that work at the gym reception says he is a first-class prick. All the young girls about 16-19 think he is great, and so does he, he is always going out with them having sex with them. A 45-year-old guy should not be dating young girls, and he is a coke head as well, the guy works making pizza now in the local pizza-shop for £8 an hour, so much for his big pop star image, eh.' Mr Sean.

Yes, Phil, he has Histrionic Personality Disorder (HPD), he wants to be the centre of attention in any group of people and he feels extremely uncomfortable when he is not, mate.'

I have seen him going into the toilets at the hotel gym, and he is in the disabled toilet snorting his cocaine off the toilet cistern, and comes out high as a kite, with a big grin on his face.

Most of the people that go down to the fitness studio, spa, at the hotel are really good people, in total there are 400 members. The wine merchant guy called Patrick, he owns a few wine shops, and he has got the wine bar in the centre of town. He employees 16 people and he is nice guy to talk to, another businessman Alan runs a factory making bulk bags and bags for seaweed, selling them all over the world, employs a lot of local people. Barry has a few garages around Tayside selling top of the range classic cars. Gordon Russell the accountant 'the more successful the people are, the more friendly they are.'

That is true Mr Sean, and you have the international airline pilot, Mark Mc shagger, he lives up to his name. He was telling me the other day that he has girls all over the world. He takes a couple of kilos of cocaine in his airline bag, while he is flying the planes, no doubt smuggling the cocaine to foreign buyers.'

How do you know that Phil, did he tell you?

No, he shook my hand, and I picked it up, I saw the picture in my head of him, placing the cocaine into his pilot carry-on bag. His friend Barry, the property developer, is building condominiums in Barcelona. The two painters and decorators, Lee and Scott, - Lee was telling me last week his wife Niamh; gave birth to a boy called Cillian, he is one year old now. Scotts partner, was due to give birth in 4 weeks, she must have had the child by now. Still, I have not seen them in ages, they are all right down to earth people, and there's the big guy Gary with the beard. He is an avid record collector and dealer, he has records from the '60s '70s 80's, worth thousands of pounds. He was a bodyguard for all the A-list celebrities down in London but gave it up to concentrate on his record collecting hobbies.'

And the other big guy from Morocco, his name is Yusuf, he is a taxi driver and a minder for the rich young people that go to St Andrews University, and the other guy Garry was working for a major supermarket in Dundee, for 31 years, but took his voluntary redundancy, he is just taking it nice and easy now, the guy called Murry he is a self-employed electrician, the retired coupe Dave and his wife Jean, Dave's an excellent swimmer, swam the river Tay many times, and Louise, she works in the chemist then the guy called Ken he is working as a private tutor, across different subjects, then there is Scott and Paddy. Scott works for some taxi firm, but I do not know what Paddy works as, that's not his real name Paddy, its because his surname is Ireland, so everyone calls him Paddy, then last, but no means least, old George 82-year-old, and Dianne, she works as a nurse, George follows her around like a puppy. I forgot to mention Colin shop keeper in St Andrews, but sold his shop and works part time as a van driver and a guy called John he works for the water board, some water technician highly skilled one. There are a lot of other girls that go down at different times, and a lot of girls come in with the day passes looking for a sugar daddy, and there are a few other good men and women that go to the health suite, but like everywhere else in life, there are a good few assholes, that act like they are prominent businessmen, but they are first-class numptys. Then you have all the female entertainers I work with, they all go down to the spa.

You have nailed it on the head there, Phil, you have described them down to T mate, but you have left out two people, Phil.'

I may not have remembered everybody, but who are you talking about?

The last time I was down at the sauna, you were not there, you must have been doing something else, do you remember the two guy's Angus and Ethan ?they are in their late 20's ? Yes I forgot about them, course I do Angus is an actor he's had a few acting roles known as 'spear-carrier 5' he has not hit the big time yet, but one day he will have a chance.' and Ethan, was he not a salesman?

He was, and he's still is a salesman, but I was talking to them the other day. Ethan used to buy and sell shares on the stock market, so some years ago when everything crashed, house prices, stock market, etc., etc., a well-known Scottish banks shares went down to 21 pence each. Now, Ethan knowing about shares, he and Angus bought a lot of the bank shares - 45,000 of them to be exact. Within four months the shares went from 21 pence per share to over £5 per share, making them a lot of money. This happened about five years ago, so the pair of them were telling me they opened up their own pizzeria shop, they sell fast-food pizza, now they have pizzeria shops in every major town in Scotland; also they have opened shops all over England and wales as well, which is some going as they are up against a lot of competitors in the fast-food trade, especially with all international fast-food franchises. Phil, you will not believe the name of the company they are trading under.

Well, give it to me, Mr Sean!

YIN YANG PIZZA'S

Their pizza has got to be the best, I never knew *yin yang pizzas was started up by two young men from Dundee, well Phil you know now, there's a lot of money to be made in the fast-food trade. And they have opened shops all over Britain. Angus and Ethan says within the next year, or so they will be the biggest pizza chain in the UK.*

They started with help from family and friends, now they employee well over 300 people in Scotland. Next year they will have over 2,000 people working for them In the UK.

That's really good news for them, Mr Sean, did they give you any pizza vouchers?

"4 hours later."

Hello, Mr Sean, you took your time answering the phone!

Sorry, Phil, I was in the shower, is that all you phoned me to say?

No, I am phoning to tell you about two bodies were found on the outskirts of Dundee. Two males. They were naked, hands tied behind their backs, and they were placed into two barrels and discovered four days ago, but the police are just going public with the information now.'

That's a bit heavy, Phil, there are only about three murders a year here in Dundee, and they are just people getting stabbed.'

Yes, I know Mr Sean, but the two guys are, well they were, two drug dealers, Sammy the *hatchet* gal *and his sidekick jimmy the weasel glen.*'

So, they must have ripped off someone, the wrong person, obviously Phil.'

Mr Sean, you know Sammy and Jimmy, were two bodybuilders and the pair of them were martial arts experts. They have some serious muscle behind them, you don't pick up two guys like of the street and bundle them in the back of a car now do you? The police say their bodies were mutilated like wild animals attacked them, and this is the clincher here Mr Sean, the pair off them had 66 nails embedded in their heads each. Police say a high power nail-gun was used. Their genitals were cut off and put into their mouths. You know as well the pair of them had connections all over Scotland in the drug trade and under-world, but nobody deserves to die slowly and painfully like that mate.

That's terrible news, Phil. You hear things like that happening in Mexico, etc., etc., but not here in Dundee. That's a message being given out to the other drug dealers in Dundee. There are new players in town, and these are guys that don't fuck about, it's a new different ball game now! Let us hope that's the last of the killings, but something tells me it's just the start of a new era, in the drug trade not only in Dundee but Scotland as well Phil. Anyway, two days we will be heading down to London for the break you won on the radio, can't wait to get out of here even it's only for a couple of days Phil.'

Yes, I know mate, tomorrow I have to go down for a course on how to fill in your CV for applying for jobs, and if I don't go, they will cut off my jobseekers allowance, for all it's worth Mr Sean but it's better than a kick in the balls with a clubfoot, mate.

So, Phil, you have some guy that's getting say about £34,000 per year telling you how to fill in your CV, about jobs that are not here.'

Yes, I know, mate, but they say that new Museum and waterfront development will create a lot of jobs, mate.'

Sure, Phil minimum wage hotel work and bar work, plus that museum is now £40 million over budget, and how many builders worked on it from Dundee?

Go on, Mr Sean enlighten me.'

No Phil and they are going to be spending over £1bn on the waterfront as well, it will look good, but I don't think it will bring too many jobs to Dundee.

Yes, I know Mr Sean, but the SNP are doing better than the rest of the political elite.'

Phil, your head's up your ass mate, if you think that, they are only doing this for votes mate, the jobs it will bring to

Dundee, will be minimum wage jobs, bar jobs, restaurant jobs, hotel jobs, etc.

AT THE AIRPORT "WE'RE ON OUR WAY TO PARADISE

The airport speaker system blares out flight announcements, and the airport comes alive with various people moving to rush to the check-in counter and others checking their flight ticket to be sure it's not their flights called. 'The 'Last call for passengers traveling on flight REB-1798 to London Heathrow, please make Your way to gate 1916, the gate will close in 20 minutes.'

'Mr Sean, that's our flight just called over the Loudspeaker.'

'Come then, Phil, let's get a move on.'

Inside the plane, a lovely looking young *air-stewardess approached us.* 'Good morning gentlemen, *please take your seats,* departure is in 15 minutes.'

'Here, Mr Sean.'

'Yes, Phil, what is it? I was just wondering, have you noticed that half of the stewardesses are young-looking, and the other ones are older?'

'Well, what that tells me, Phil, is that the younger ones are just learning to become a stewardess and the older girls are training them, the older ones have been on planes all around the world, ok.'

'Yes, sure, Mr Sean.'

Here Mr Sean, have you noticed the two Asian guys sitting at the front of the plane?'

No Phil,why? I don't look at everybody all the time, now do I.'

It's just all the passengers who are getting on the plane are giving them suspicious looks.'

Phil dinnae be worrying about them, we have just passed the most stringent security check any airport has to offer mate. It's not like they have just walked through all that security with suicide belts on is it? Anyway you start to worry when we're halfway through the flight and they stand to shout, *ALLAHU AKBAR*, Then you know you're up shit creek without a paddle, and the plane is going down Phil.

Why shout ALLAHU AKBAR, (GOD IS GREAT) THEN BLOW YOURSELF UP?, MOST OF THE SUICIDE BOMBERS ARE PROMISED 40 VIRGINS IN THE AFTERLIFE, and THEY HAVE MORE CHANCE GROWING TWO HEADS, THAN GETTING 40 VIRGINS HERE On EARTH, THAN IN THE AFTERLIFE.

'Good morning ladies and gentlemen, this is Captain Cotton speaking. We will be flying at the altitude of 25,000 feet, our flight time will be 1 hour 30 minutes. I'd like to thank you once again for choosing Air Finger's. The cabin crew will see to your needs. Cabin crew prepare for take-off. Here we go, scum-dee men, on tour.'

'Yes, Mr Sean, London, here we come.'

Sean adjusted in his seat, thinking to himself. Somebody sitting behind our seats must have had beans for their breakfast, they were farting like a pig, the whole plane was stinking! Best of all, the plane's two toilets was always engaged. I think the air stewardesses just locked them for a joke and were watching the passenger reactions on the closed-circuit TV while sitting at the back of the plane. They have them in all the aircraft now due to the threat of terrorism, and some off-air flight attendant has had training in the use of stun guns. I wish they used their stun gun on that guy sitting behind me with the blue suit on, he's the one that's farting, sitting there with a big grin on his face, he must like the smell of his farts !!!!!!

'This is Captain Cotton, we will be landing in 10 minutes, cabin crew prepare for landing, once again I like to thank you for flying with Air Finger's.'

The cabin crew did their usual checks, making sure all the passengers had their seatbelts on. It's good looking out of the window, descending through the thick white clouds. And there it is, London town about 1,000 feet below, everything looks small from up here. Big Ben, the Houses of Parliament, London Eye. The runway zooms up in front of you, touch down imminent.

How come planes always seem to take forever taxiing to it a final place where the passenger can disembark?

The guy that was sitting behind my seat was now walking as if he had just come off the back of a horse, hahaha, he's shit himself, that will teach him to be so disgusting.

'Here, Phil, go and tap him on the shoulder and ask him if he needs to go to the toilet now.'

'Mr Sean, Ok, that's no probs. Here excuse me sir, but I think you have "shit" your boxer shorts.'

That was funny; he never knew where to look, he's red as a beetroot now, it would be even funnier if he gets a strip search from customs.

We are now waiting at the carousel, to pick up our suitcases and go through customs, *is it me? Or do the custom officers ask some daft Questions?*

'Passport please, Sir.' 'Here you are, officer.'

'Mr Sean, it a very unusual name.' 'Yes, it is.' *See page one*

'Did you pack your suitcase yourself, sir.' 'Indeed, I did officer.' 'Have you at any time left your suitcase unattended sir.' 'Only once, I had to check it in officer.' 'Has anybody asked you to take anything with you on the plane.' 'No, sir, I replied.' *He's beginning to piss me off now with all these Questions'*

'Have you ever taken any drugs.' 'No officer, only prescription medicine from my doctor.'

'Do you know of anybody, or have you met anybody that has taken drugs?'

'That must be the stupidest question anybody has asked me; I come from Dundee, half of Dundee, are on drugs , marijuana, heroin, ecstasy, cocaine, tablets, glue, etc., etc., etc.'

'Just answer the question, sir.' 'Well, it has to be "yes" then, officer!'

He knew he's was pissing me off now, and he loved it.

'I will take a swab of your hand and inside of your suitcase now, sir.'

'Yes, sure officer, help yourself. *I bet everyone at school bullied him. That was why he was being an asshole now.*

'I will now go and put the swab into the puffer machine, and please wait here, sir.'

'Yeah, go for it, officer.'

Puffer machine is an explosive trace-detection portal machine, also known as a trace portal machine. It is a security device that seeks to detect explosives and illegal drugs at airports and other sensitive facilities as part of airport security screening.

'Thank you for your time, sir, you are now free to go, have a lovely stay in London.'

'Ye sure will do officer.' *fucking prick!*

'Here Phil, are we getting a taxi to the hotel.' 'No Mr Sean, all I have to do is to phone this number, and we will be picked up by a chauffeured stretch limousine and transported to our hotel, Mr Sean.'

'Sure Phil, you're always 'well organised Phil.' 'Yeah better to be organised, than not, Mr Sean.'

Twenty minutes later, Phil and I were dropped off outside this big hotel, and the hotel porter was taking our suitcases up to our rooms.

'Here, Mr Sean, we will go out early tomorrow and go sightseeing.'

'Ye sure Phil, I want to go and see the Waxwork's, that's all I want to see here in London.'

'Cool, see you in the morning then.' 'Yeah sure, Mr Sean.'

Later, in the dining room. 'Good morning, gentlemen, the breakfast is self-service , if you have any dietary requirements, please ask one of the waiting staff.'

'OK then, thank you very much for pointing that out to myself and my colleague.'

'Why are you talking like that Mr Sean.' 'All part of the bullshit Phil.'

'Yeah, here's me thinking you're going all upper class on me, Mr Sean.'

'That would not be hard, Phil, now would it?' 'Cheers to that, Mr Sean.'

'I am only joking, Phil.' 'Yes, I know you are, you f*cking twat.'

'Excuse me Miss, may I order four vegetarian sausages, two pieces, of toast and a cold glass of milk.

'Yes sir, said the waitress, I will place your order with the chef and help yourself to the toast and milk, this is a self-service breakfast, sir.' Said the waitress.

I looked at her as she was walking away. 'F*ck, if she smiles, her face will crack, she's got a face like Myra Hindley' that's been licking dog's piss off a bunch "o" Jaggie nettles.'

she's probably working for minimum wage and having to put on a show for all the people that come here for breakfast.'

The waitress came across to the table with the glasses of milk, she touched Phil on the shoulder, while she placed the milk down. Phil turned and looked her in the eyes and said congratulations, have you chosen a name for the baby? The waitress looked astonished, and said she and her partner, have been trying for a baby for three years now. Phil replied well you are pregnant now. And sure enough, she came over to Phil the next day and said, last night after work she went into the chemist, and bought a pregnancy test kit, and had a positive result, I am 4 weeks pregnant she told Phil and kissed him on the right side of his face, and said, am I having a boy or girl?

Phil replied, both you are having twins.'

I have known you all my life Phil and that's the second time I have seen you do that mate;! That's the sixth sense, big boy, anyway what was I going to say, I remember now, 'Here, Mr Sean, I could never be a vegetarian. I like my meat too much.'

'Yeah, Phil, that's what your sister said, she could never be a vegetarian, no Phil, she says she likes her meat too much.'

'Yeah, Mr Sean, you will never know after the Waxworks, we can go back to the hotel, have a shower and freshen up, then go to the Smoo gig. Later we can go back to the club where there will be a celebration for the end of the world tour, that sounds good to me Phil.'

'That gig was like watching five "OAPs" singing and dancing for three hours; I never thought it was any good.'

'Yeah, Mr Sean, but it never cost us anything, remember?'

'Yeah, I know Phil, it's better if you don't pay for it, and it's off to the club in an hour, this should be good, keep your fingers-crossed.'

'Here Mr Sean, I got a phone call from the main desk, the limo will be outside in ten minutes.'

'Ok, Phil, I will see you down in the lobby.'

'Driver, can you drop my colleague and me off around the corner from the club.'

'Yes Sir, I will do that for you, have a lovely time gentleman.' 'Sure, will have a good time, cheers mate.' Walking around the corner, all the "*PAPARAZZI*" were there trying to get the one photo that will pay them hundreds, if not thousands of pounds for the right ones.

'Have you got the invitations.' 'Sure, I do, Mr Sean.' 'Here they are, one for you and one for me.'

The chief doorman was taking the invitations, he was the size of a mountain, about 6'11 inches high.

I would rather fight him than feed him' Phil, he's a big bastard.

'Yeah, Mr Sean, I was thinking that myself.

Inside the place was full of A-list celebs, singers, actors, if you were famous, you would be here.

I pointed in the direction of two people sitting at a table, 'Look there, that is that actor "Brad Smitt" with his ex "Jennifer" she's a great actress, and so is Brad, she's so lovely looking, feck it, I'm going to ask her for a dance.'

'There is no way in hell she's dancing with you, and you have got more chance of Brad doing backflips, mate.'

'Watch and learn, Phil, watch and lean,'

So, Phil's watching me speak to Brad and Jennifer, and the next *thing he knows is I am dancing with her.*

'Eh Phil, so what you think about that? Phil, whose is DA's man? Phil, whose DA's man?'

'You are Mr Sean; you're DA, man.'

'So, Mr Sean, are you going to tell me?' 'Tell you what Phil?'

'Tell me how the hell you got Jennifer to dance with you?' 'I'll tell you after Phil, ok.'

'Yeah, sure.'

'Mr Sean, I was waiting for you to start stripping when you were on the dance floor.'

'If I did that, Phil, there would be a riot with all the girls in here.' 'Yeah, Mr Sean, you're full of it.'

'I am going to the toilet Phil, I'll be back in a couple of minutes.'

The toilets didn't have urinals, it had about 20 cubicles and each has its toilet, wash hand sink, and that one for cleaning your arse, what's it called again? *I needed that*, as I was washing my hands, I saw a watch on the side of the sink. Not just any watch, it was heavy, made of gold and encrusted with diamonds.

I took it out with me to show Phil. Why are you walking like that, Mr Sean? I have pee down my bloody leg, but look at this Phil.' 'Wow, what a lovely watch Mr Sean, here, it has got some writing on the back of it, it says "to my nephew and namesake from *Pablo Escobar*

'I've heard that name before Phil, "Pablo Escobar," I don't know where, but it will come back to me.'

'We'll take it to the security staff and ask if we can see the manager.' *Phil replied.*

'I am not handing it to any security staff as it may disappear, you know what I am saying, Phil?'

'Of course, I do, Mr Sean.'

Bar staff pointed us toward the manager – a casually dressed guy, stood chatting and laughing with guests.

'Good evening, gentlemen, I am Mr Tony Rogers, the manager of the club, how can I help you? 'Well, when I was in the toilet's I found this watch, we feel it is a very expensive watch, it's got a name at the back of it, "Pablo Escobar."'

'I know this gentleman, he's the new owner of this night club, leave it with me, and I will make sure he gets it back.'

***

'What do you think? You think he will hand it back.'

Yeah, he will, that's his new boss. About 15 minutes later, the manager was talking to this woman and pointing over to where we were sitting.

'Here, Phil, here she comes.'

As she came into my focus, wow, I could not help but admire how lovely she looks, long black hair, hourglass figure, olive skin, about 5,6 tall a real classy looking lady.

I knew she liked me as soon as she laid eyes on me, her eyes glazed. I am good at reading women's body language, you must be, being a male stripper. Two bodyguards accompanied her, all the men in the place are watching her from the corner of their eyes as she walks across the floor.

'Good evening, gentlemen, my name is Maria. I am Pablo Escobar's "PA," personal assistant.

'Hello Maria, I am Mr Sean, and this is Phil.' 'Mr Sean, an unusual name.' said Maria, *(see page one)*

'Pablo would like to thank you personally for being so kind in handing in his watch, please follow me, gentlemen.'

'Don Pablo, these are the two gentlemen who found your watch, this is Mr Sean, and this is Phil.'

Pablo looks up to take a closer look at us from his seat. 'Why thank you very much for being so virtuous and giving my watch to the manager, this watch means so much to me as it was a gift from my uncle, Pablo Escobar before the search block murdered him.'

(Search block was a specially chosen police force in Columbia, with one purpose, to find and kill Pablo Escobar.

The American government wanted him to be extradited, to spend the rest of his life behind bars in the US.

He had the blood of thousands of people on his hands, police, judges, political figures, innocent people like me and you, he took no prisoners in his war with the Colombian government and, in turn, with the US government as well. In the '80s, it all had to do with one thing "cocaine". He was the biggest and most brutal of all the drug lords in all Columbia; he was the first narco-terrorist).

'I will not go into details about this tragic time in my and my family's life, please come and join me, have a seat Mr Sean, Phil.'

Don Pablo was like any other guy, wore jeans, white training shoes, white tee-shirt. Apart from the thick gold chain around his neck and, of course, the gold watch he wore, he also had black curly hair with a Mexican style moustache. He has a dark complexion, well, he had to since he is from Columbia.

He looks like that American actor that took the part of the P.I. in the '80s, you know him, he drove that red Ferrari 308 GTB, Tom...forgot his surname name, but it will come back to me later on.

***

'Tell me, Mr Sean, what line of business do you do? maybe we can work something out, Mr Sean, an unusual name.' *Said Don Pablo.*

'no, Don Pablo, we are not businessmen, we had won this trip on a local radio competition to see the rock band "the Smoo" and to come here for their farewell party, we do not work, we are both unemployed guys from a place called Dundee. So, Don Pablo, what line of business are you into?'

'Well, Mr Sean, I am into "export."' '*Exporting* what Don Pablo?'

Pablo kept quiet for a few seconds, breathes in and out, and responds. 'Well gentlemen, it is time for me to retire for the night. In two weeks, I will be in Monaco to watch my racing team compete in the F1, would you and Phil like to join me as my guests back in Columbia for a two week holiday, just a token of my goodwill and to say thank you for handing back my watch. My plane can easily make the detour and pick yourself and Phil up at the nearest airport where you live.'

(*F*CKING SOUND CARPEDIEM*)

'Why, yes, Don Pablo, if it can be arranged, we would love to visit Colombia, as your guests.'

'So, let it be.' Replied Don Pablo.

'Dundee is just like any other city or town in the UK, it has a major drug problem. All you have to do is to go to any chemist, first thing in the morning, and you will see the junkies getting their methadone to ween them of the heroin. They have to take it in front of the chemist because some of the junkies were not swallowing it,' but going outside and spitting it into a plastic bottle to resell it, *"you must be a right sad bastard, to buy methadone from a druggie and it costs the Scottish government £40,000 per year. There's an epidemic of cocaine, not only in Britain but worldwide. A staggering 85% of men and women between the age of 18-53 are addicted to Pablo's cocaine"*

'Please leave your details with Maria.' 'Yes, Don Pablo, I will take down their details.'

As she looked at me with a big, beautiful smile, I've never seen a smile so beautiful in my life. 'Maria, can I ask you a question.' 'Yes, Mr Sean.'

'Who is the guy that stands behind Pablo Escobar and watches his every move and the moves of everybody around him.'

Maria's smile as always, 'His name is "Mamould Abdelsamie," he is Pablo Escobars top lieutenant of his elite sicario's, (Columbian hitmen) . All Pablo Escobar has to do is to look at him the right way and he will take care of that person. Mamould Abdelsamie would lay down his life, as would all of Pablo Escobar Sicarios. The other guys are Blackie, Poison, Scorpion, Jose, Esteban, Juan Felipe, Yerson; these are Don Pablo main men.'

(f*ck, I am not even going to look Mamould Abdelsamie in the eyes) 'Mahmoud Abdelsamie does not sound like a Columbian, name Maria.'

No, Mr Sean, he came from Egypt, from a place called Hurghada, he worked in one of Pablo Escobars hotels. He was a guest relation manager there before he came over to work with the elite sicarios, he is a very nice man to talk to, as you will get to find out Mr Sean, Phil.'

'Well Maria, I will go over and thank Pablo Escobar and say good night, I look for forward to seeing you again, Maria.'

'Yes, Mr Sean, I look forward to the next time we will meet again, Mr Sean, Phil, good night.'

'Well, thank you for an evening of entertainment, and your kind hospitality Don Pablo.'

'It's time for myself and Phil to shoot the crow.' 'What is this, to shoot the crow, Mr Sean?'

'Sorry, Don Pablo, it's just a saying back home in Dundee, it just means it is also time for myself and Phil to go back to the hotel.'

Back at the hotel the next morning at breakfast.

'Mr Sean, I've checked that guy out, Don Pablo.'

'And what Phil?'

'He's the "head of the Olmec cartel" named after the first civilization to settle in pre-Columbian, and he's the richest man in the world. He is the number one cocaine exporter in the world, and he launders money through his businesses making him even more money. As for the cocaine, he exports 85%, and that mainly goes to the USA. Worldwide, he also owns airline companies, gold mines, diamond mines, F1 racing group's, and for his daughter's 21st birthday present, he bought her the clothing design company "renniearenoos," and he paid $2 billion for it. He owns hotel chains all over the world, he's got all his drug money invested in everything that money can buy, banks, etc., etc., you name it, he will have money invested in it, or he will own it. He employs 4 million people worldwide, and his political party is the leading party in Columbia, so there no extradition. The USA would like to see him behind bars for the rest of his life. Pablo Escobar was not only the richest man in the world but very intelligent as well, the only people that don't like him is the American government, because of the people that take cocaine over there in the USA and take a guess, how much money he makes per week?

'Phil, I don't know just tell me, I've no time for playing guessing games.'

'What's up with you Mr Sean, did you get up on the wrong side of the bed this morning?'

'Sorry, Phil, sorry for being snappy at you, tell me.' 'He earns $ 1 billion per week every week, and he has diplomatic immunity worldwide, so he has no fear of being deported to the USA.'

'That's some wage packet, Phil, to get $1 billion per week.' 'Well, that's what it says on the internet and in that American magazine that does all the richest people in the world. Who knows, maybe he owns that as well. His private plane is the 747-8, one of the biggest passenger planes in the world, it cost him $500 million to buy and $200 million to customize, wow, that must be some plane Phil.'

'You are right it will be and that the plane that we will be getting picked up in, it's got a gym, steam- room, hot tubs, sauna, cinema, four of the world's finest chefs, and 40 full-time crew.

'This is going to be some two week holiday over in Colombia. I don't think he'll fly the both of us back on his private plane, there is no need to, remember he owns an airline company, he'll just book two tickets one-way back to scum-dee.' 'Yeah right Mr Sean.'

All of his sicarios must be multi-millionaires.' yeah I ken Phil, are you thinking about asking him for a job?

No, I am just making conversation, big-boy, come into my room, I have a vape e-cigarette on charge I just bought it the other day. As *Phil sits at the table putting this vape cigarette together,* Phil there's must be about six different pieces to this vape cigarette, you look like Francisco Scaramanga putting that vape cigarette together mate.'

(K) Mr Sean, who is Franceso Scaramanga?

He was the baddie in the film The Man With The Golden Gun, remember when he was sitting speaking to Bond, while he was putting together the lighter, cigarette-case, and the pen was the muzzle of the golden gun.

Yeah, I remember it. I have not seen that film in ages, Mr Sean and remember, we fly back tomorrow, is there anything else you want to do or see here in London? 'No, I am just going to chill out for the day, we can go down to the bar and chill out there, have a couple of drinks.' 'That's fine by me, Mr Sean.'

Look Mr Sean there's that London hardman Danny Dyers, he's sitting drinking wine with his daughter. She's a lovely looking girl, she's always on tv he does a lot of documentaries, what his favourite saying again, *"go on my son,"* I am going to go over and introduce myself, Mr Sean.' Phil dinnae be daft mate, you are just going over to have a look-see at his daughter. What do you think she'll say, daddy, daddy, I want a scots man as a pet please buy me one please. You have more chance sticking your arse out the window, and running downstairs and throwing stones at it mate than his daughter looking at you Phil, anyway, he's not a hard man Phil, how many hard men do you see drinking wine with a straw and a cocktail umbrella in his glass, he's a "Pricks, prick."

Scanning the lounge with my eyes. 'Look, there are two blonde girls over there, Phil.'

'The two girls are beautiful, Mr Sean.'

The two blondes.............will be thick as mince.............*thick as mince is a saying in Scotland, meaning the person or persons are stupid.*

'Phil, how do you know if a blonde got a vibrator.' 'I don't know Mr Sean.' 'Because she will have chipped teeth.' '(K) Mr Sean.' 'Phil, it's a joke, think about it! You were at the back of the queue when God was giving out brains, weren't you?'

'I get it now, Mr Sean.' 'Nice one.'

'The two girls are about the same age as you and I, watch and learn Phil, follow my lead.'

I approach the ladies with my good luck charming smile. 'hello ladies, my colleague and I would like to buy the two prettiest girls in London a drink, what would the pair of you like to drink ?, 'Thank you very much; we will have two Moscow mule's cocktails. one memento please.'

'Ladies excuse my ignorance, ladies, my name is Doctor Sean, and the person to my left is Doctor Phil, we are here in London for a conference on advanced emergency trauma surgery.'

'Fascinating gentlemen, my name is Jean, and this is my best friend Samantha, Sammy for short. We are celebrating passing our Ph.D. (doctor of philosophy) in quantum mechanics and securing positions in the European space agency.'

(OOPPS)

'My colleague and I do wish the pair of you all the best with your new jobs.

'Phil its time, we must be at the conference, we are sorry, but we need to go now ladies, bye.'

'Yeah sure, Mr Sean, "thick as mince."' 'Just keep walking, Phil.'

'Well, that fell flat on its face Mr Sean, Ph.D. in quantum mechanics.' 'You know what Robert the Bruce said, "If at first you don't succeed, try, try again."' 'Yeah, Mr Sean, but not with blondes!' 'feck off Phil.'

Well, it's better than you, the last girls you were talking to, you told them that you were a trainee gynaecologist, but you had to give it up because you were scared of the dark, but if they liked you will check them over and have a wee look-see.

I was only joking with them, Mr Sean.'

Yes, I know you were mate, but they never saw the funny side of it, after they called you a pervert and one of them gave you a backhander and burst your lip.'

Don't I know it, Mr Sean I still have the scar from her fecking ring, on the side of my nose and lip.

***

Next day, waiting at the airport departure lounge. 'Remember Phil, don't tell anyone that we've been invited over to Columbia by the biggest drug kingpin and the richest man in the world, not even your sister Shirley.' 'Yes sure, Mr Sean, I will not tell anybody.' 'Good Phil.' 'And that goes for you to Mr Sean, don't tell your brothers, bri (Brian) or Tone (Tony).' 'Yeah, I know Phil, remember the old saying.' 'What's that?' *Phil asked with a puzzled look on his face.*

'Never let the right hand know what the left hand is doing.' 'I've never heard that saying before, Mr Sean.' 'Well, you learn something new every day, Phil.' 'Hmmmmm.'

'I don't think that will come in handy anyway, and it will not be long before we are back in boring scum-dee.' 'Yeah, but in two weeks, we'll be flying high in Pablo Escobars own f*cking private plane to Columbia.'

'Now, that's something to look forward to, eh.

'We'll have to remember Phil; it's a different culture from the one here, and no taking any drugs.'

Yeah, I know, Mr Sean.' 'No way, we'll just go and enjoy ourselves, kick back and relax, have some fun and hopefully meet some nice girls.'

'Yeah, Mr Sean, like the ones we meet in the club.' 'well, I got a dance from Jennifer.'

'Yes, that was a class act to follow Mr Sean, so how did you get her to dance with you.'

'I'll tell you, later, Phil, ok.'

"Three days later"

Godmother of cocaine I have been reading up about the Colombian drug cartels, from a book I got from the liberty.'

well, what did you find out about them, big boy?

Well, I am going to tell you Phil, and knock that on the head calling me big boy, don't call me that out in Colombia. In the 70's there was a woman named Gresalda, she was from Colombia but lived in the USA in New York, *she was the godmother of cocaine. S*he was a drug-smuggler, and she had a lot of people murdered. Her favourite method of torturing and murdering females that crossed her, was to have her henchmen chop up the hottest chili in the world the *"Carolina reaper chili"* and insert the chili's into the woman's vagina causing severe burning, and pain to the victim, this would be repeated throughout five (5) days of torture. If that was not bad enough, the woman *uterus was* cut out, and her breast removed, *no doubt already dead,* then the victim's throat would be cut from ear to ear. Griselda and her henchmen were the most ruthless killers in America, in the '70s. It all came to an end when she was sent to prison for 20 years in America, after her release, she returned to Colombia, where one day while leaving the hairdressers, she was gunned down, in broad daylight. No doubt by other drug cartel members or by relatives of her victims. *The males that were murdered by her henchmen were shot dead. Then there was the Cali cartel* this cartel was active in the 1980s, the founder was the Rodrigues Orejuela brothers, with Jose Santacruz Londono, *aka chepe, a Russian gangster convicted of helping to sell the Cali cartel a Russian submarine in the '90s.* They were based in Colombia around the city Cali, they supplied drug around the Americas, the Cali cartel was that big Phil, they spent $1 BN per year paying off police, judges, army, you name it. If you could help the Cali cartel you would be on their payroll, but if you refused you would be shot, they had everyone on their side. If a person came into Colombia they had a back ground check done on the person before their suitcases were unpacked. They were called the Cali KGB, the Cali cartel, they never went to showrooms to buy cars, they had their sicarios fly over to Germany to buy 20 Mercedes Benz cars, and have them delivered to Colombia in under 48 hour via a cargo plane. They did this all the time buying Mercedes, Lamborghinis, Ferraris, Porsches, they even got helicopters from Russia. When the USSR collapsed, you could buy anything you wanted from them, planes, tanks, etc., etc. you were buying top technology at rock bottom prices. If the cartels wanted it they would buy it, the Cali cartel as with the other drug cartels in Colombia were fighting for control of the drug routes. Colombia was a narco state divided into two, the Medellin cartel in the north, and the Cali cartel in the south each cartel had their own patch. They had rules. New York belonged to the Cali cartel, and Los Angeles belonged to the Medellin cartel. Miami and Houston were shared cites where both could enter and this was always respected. The Cali cartel had a different way of doing business, bribing people. Pablo only feared one thing and that was been extradited to the USA this is how Pablo declared war on the government and the Cali cartel, it was all out war. Pablo's sicarios set of lots of bombs, killing lots of innocent people. He also killed 457 police officers paying each person that killed a policeman $1,000,000. He also threatened members of the Cali family, "the war was on". It was no more Mr nice guys of Cali. You sees to the outside the brother were just successful businessmen, because they hid their cocaine empire through legitimate companies. The Cali cartel then turned to the son of a Colombian general, that provided mercenaries to the Colombian government before, *Jorge salcedo* 1993, *salcedo* flew in his band of mercenaries soldiers from special forces from around the world. 12 men in all, their mission was to kill Pablo Escobar, the price was $8 million. Operation Phoenix was on. The Cali cartel armed them with no expense spared weapons, M16, aris, AR 15 Zulu grenades, hand grenades. It was a waiting game. The mercenaries had a helicopter painted in nice Colombian police green, they knew once they had landed at Hacienda Napoles *Pablo main residence* ,Pablo sicarios would not go down without a fight. The mercenaries were playing toy soldiers amongst themselves in there hide-out in the jungle of Colombia. The brothers had a web of informers that had located Pablo sitting having coffee by his pool. The hired guns set off in a helicopter for Pablo, but two hours into the flight the helicopter crashed into a foggy dew hillside, killing the Colombian pilot and badly injuring *some "of the killer for money team " OPERATION PHOENIX FAILED.*

If you could help the Cali cartel in any way you would be on their payroll, and if you refused you would be dead, the drug cartels are unremorseful, to any person that gets in their way, killing and torture is an everyday occurrence in the cartels drug world. Violence poured from the hands of the drug cartels in the '80s and '90s. Cali cartel would buy a plane for $ 1.000.000, and load it with $100.000.000 worth of cocaine then fly it to Miami airstrip, unload the cocaine then leave the aircraft, that's how good the profits were. They did this week in week out, month after month, year after year, they made $7 billion a year.

The Cali cartel then joined up with the unlikely partner Colombian state. The Cali cartel informers was incredible, they had even tapped Pablo's phone, the brothers interacted with the search block, they moved in - shooting dead Pablo Escobar on a rooftop in Medellin, Colombia.

The Colombian government and the DEA, then turned their attention to the Cali cartel, *"ALL THE CARTELS GET FUCKED THE BROTHERS ARE NOW SERVING 30 YEAR EACH IN A USA JAIL".* *the cartels in the '80s would kill hundreds of people to kill one person, that's how ruthless these cartels were and all in the name of cocaine and money. They were also known as Los Pepes, made up of the enemies of Pablo Escobar, head of the Median cartel. They waged war even though it was small in the 1990's they killed anyone who had allegiance to Pablo, sicarios, accountants, lawyers, no doubt with the help of the Colombian government, which in turn had the backing of the CIA, AND DEA. Mobiles phones were not heard of in the 80's. America used to have spy planes circling*

Medellin in Colombia, trying to pick up their most wanted man using his satellite phone, Pablo Escobar. But it was the Cali cartels information, which lead to a gun battle with the search block, and ultimately his downfall on 2nd December 1993.

Phil, I can go on, and on and on, they were lots of people in the cocaine trade in Colombia, but the most powerful drug cartel in Colombia was Pablo Escobar's Medellin drug cartel.

Some people say he was ruthless and was a murderer that killed scores of people. Others say he was just protecting his business assets. *I suppose you can say just like the world-famous soft drinks company, Alleging that the company's locally owned bottlers in Colombia used paramilitary groups to kill up to Ten (10)Trade union representatives, and workers, have a coke and a smile!*

Also the big British oil company, you all know the one I am talking about, are allegedly *blamed for violating Human rights in Colombia, using paramilitary groups to kidnap and torture a Colombian Trade union Leader in 2002, all in it for one thing - money.*

The Medellin cartel bought an island in the Bahamas, and they paid the President of the Bahamas $5 million a month. This island was the trampoline for the cartel, to get their cocaine into the USA every week, boats and small yachts would arrive from Miami and be loaded with cocaine daily, To produce 1 kilo of cocaine in the jungle cost $1,000, and to transport it costs $4,000, so in total $5,000, that same kilo of cocaine in Miami in the '80s was going for $80'000, so *the daily profits were $188,000,000 (if you do the maths - your returns were in the $billions, that's how they became the largest cocaine empire in the world. They never counted the money, they weighed it. $7 million fitted into one 60 litre barrel, and the Medellin cartel was buying 400 barrels per month. The money they were making was incalculable, and Pablo soon climbed his way to the top drug pile in the world; he was the head drug trafficker in Colombia for 17 years, but before the drugs, he was selling cigarettes and stealing motor cars. Some people say he was also stealing headstones from the graves of the dead, and sanding down the names and reselling them, but there is no truth in that, just some people trying to blacken his name.*

After Pablo's failed attempt to join the Colombian government because he had a criminal record, Pablo then killed the publisher who published his mug-shot in the local paper and to finish the job he blew up the newspaper's offices (it was the mug-shot that got him kicked out of the government) This is how ruthless Pablo was in the 80's - a waiter once stole silver knives and forks from the dinner table, where Pablo was entertaining his guests. Pablo duct-taped the waiters hands and feet together and threw him into the swimming pool and watched him drown.Pablos drug cartel was unremorseful to any person who got ins their way, torture and killing was an everyday occurrence in the drug world. But if the cartels wanted to keep someone on ice, hidden in the Colombian jungle they would turn to the pro's FARC for a hefty fee, of course, they were the masters of hiding in the jungle. FARC was fighting the longest civil war in modern-day history. At the start FARC would kidnap

Colombian rich People knowing only too well that wealthy families would pay a lot of money to get their loved ones back.

The cartels never gave a shit about public relations, if they didn't shoot other cartel members, they would use chainsaws on them cutting the legs, arms, and heads off, and send them back in boxes. Sometimes 15 people from the warring cartel would die this way, the cartels never gave a fuck about human life.

Avianca Flight 203, November 27th, 1989 Presidential candidate, Cesar Gaviria, had declared war on the drug cartels in Colombia, and he and his entourage were due to be on the plane Avianca Flight 203. Still, he was informed of an assassination attempt, which was due to take place on the afore mentioned flight, so never got on, but what they forgot to do was to tell the 101 passengers and six crew members, in all 107 would die from a bomb blast on the plane "good old uncle Sam."

Gaviria became president of Colombia from 1990 to 1994.

TWO WEEKS LATER

Come on, Phil, answer your phone. 'Hello, hey Phil, Mr Sean.'

'Here, yeah, what up.' 'I've just got an email from Maria, Don Pablo's PA. 'And what?' 'Don't tell me they can't make it?' 'No Phil, they will be here tomorrow at 1 pm, but they cannot land at the Dundee airport because it's too small so they will be at the bigger international airport in the capital.'

'Ok, Mr Sean, so do we make our way there?'

'No, Maria is sending Don Pablo's personal chauffeur to pick the pair of us up.'

'Cool Mr Sean.' 'And the car will be a Bugatti Chiron sports car.'

'Wow, that's some car Mr Sean, but are they not a two-seater sports car, 'Yeah, I asked Maria, she says Pablo Escobar had one specially made into a five-seater car, not bad if you're the richest man in the world, Phil.'

'That must have cost him millions of dollars.' 'Yeah Phil, pocket change to him.'

'Too right, Mr Sean, so come up to my house with your suitcase, and we will wait for the Chauffeur and Mahmoud Abdelsamie will be with the chauffeur.'

'What's is he coming for? I don't know Phil, maybe to keep the driver company.'

'Yeah, did you give them your address and postcode for the satellite navigation system, 'What do you think? I am fecking stupid Phil; they had it anyway, Maria was checking to see if it was ok and check if there were any mistakes.'

'There's the car parking outside my house, and here is the chauffeur coming to pick up our suitcases, this is the life Phil, they say money can't buy happiness, yeah but it helps Mr Sean.

'This is a lovely looking car, Chi-co, that's the chauffeur's name, he said it is one of the best cars he has ever driven.' (*Lucky bastard, he's gets paid for driving all don Pablo's cars*).

'Mahmoud Abdelsamie, can I ask you something? 'Yes, of course, Mr Sean.'

'What would you like to know?' 'You were working in a hotel in Egypt?' 'Yes, that's is correct, Mr Sean.'

'So, why are you working as Pablo Escobar top lieutenant of his sicarios?'

'Money Mr Sean, I would have to live a 100 lifetimes to earn what I earn here in one week, I have worked for Pablo Escobar for 15 years now, I am very happy to be serving Don Pablo.'

'This is a personal question, Mahmoud, but have you ever taken someone's life?'

'Mr Sean, please, you ask too many questions, let's say a carpenter sharpens his tool because he always uses them.' 'Yes, ok, Mahmoud, I know what you are saying.'

'We will be at the airport in 13 minutes, please have your passports ready for inspection, I would like to tell you one thing you need to know Mr Sean, Phil, Don Pablo has three daughters, please, please, please, do not look at them with lust in your eyes, he is unduly protective of his daughters.'

'Don't worry, Mahmoud, we are just here for 14 days holiday, that's all, we would never disrespect Don Pablo.'

After all the security checks at the airport.

'Wow, look at the size of this plane, f*ck it's humongous.'

'Well, it's one of the world's biggest passenger planes, Phil.' And there she was, standing at the door of the plane.

'Maria, good afternoon Mr Sean, Phil, welcome aboard.'

'Wow Maria, you look stunningly beautiful, if waves in the ocean measured good looks, you would be a Tsunami.'

'Thank you, Mr Sean, compliments flow from your mouth like honey that has poured out of a jar.'

And here he is, Don Pablo, sitting on a leather seat like the king of the castle.

'Pleased to meet you don Pablo.' 'Welcome aboard, Mr Sean, Phil, he said, sitting with his white dressing gown on.'

Don Pablo looks like an American actor, that played the part of Magnum P.I. Tom Selwick, I think that his name anyway.

An announcement came from the pilot. 'Take off will be in ten minutes.'

Don Pablo shifted a bit in his seat. 'Please make yourself at home, gentlemen.'

'Phil and I have brought you a wee gift from scum-dee, a bottle of scotch whiskey and some shortbread biscuits homemade by my mum's next-door neighbour, Tina; she's a lovely cook and baker Don Pablo.'

'Thank you, and I have a gift for yourself and Phil too.' *Don Pablo hands over a small box to us, inside each was a gold and diamond ring each, these are gold and diamond rings!*

'These are no ordinary rings, these diamonds come from the deepest diamond mines in the world, they are from Botswanan in Africa. The diamonds are the rarest ones in the world, yellow, and red diamonds, you can't buy these rings anywhere. I have had my jeweller make these rings for yourself and Phil, if one could buy them, they would cost between two to three to buy.'

'Thank you very much, Don Pablo.

***

'No, no, no, Mr Sean, two to three million of your British pounds.'

'Thank you, Don Pablo, your generosity is beyond belief. (As *soon as I get home, I am taking this down to Hatton gardens in London to sell and will be set up for the rest of my life).*

'I will always wear it, and every time I look at it, I will think of you.' (*Yeah right*) 'Please, please, Mr Sean, Phil, don't insult my intelligence, I know as soon as you're back home, you will sell these ring's and live a good comfortable life, a ring is an unbroke circle, it has no story or history.

'!!!! a man got to live don Pablo; men got to live !!!!'

'Please take a seat and get ready for take-off, gentlemen.'

'Yes, sure, Don Pablo.' 'Hey, Phil.' 'Yeah, what up Mr Sean?' 'Nothing.'

'I was just going to tell you that the seasonal job I was doing last year with the council as a Park Ranger is coming up again, and it's mine if I want it, starts next month.'

'Good Mr Sean, when you come back from Columbia, you've got a job to come back to.'

'Yeah, sure Phil.' *if only I knew what lay ahead of myself and Phil.*

'You are now free to take off your seatbelts, gentlemen.' Maria said, 'You like her, Mr Sean, do you?' 'Yeah, Phil, she's is beautiful. I am going to get to know her better before this trip is over.'

'Go for it Mr Sean, I know she likes you too, she keeps on looking over at you.'

'Well, tell you one thing, Phil, she's got a good taste.'

Just play it cool; your time will come. (Tiofaidh ar la) 'Mr Sean, Phil, please let me show you around my plane.' 'Yeah, sure, Don Pablo.'

'This plane is like a flying hotel, and it has everything, gym, hot tubs, sauna, bars, it's even got a dance floor.' all the floors had pearl carpets of Baroda, and all the walls have white pin cushion leather. 'You sure know how to live the good life, Don Pablo.'

'Yes, indeed, I do, Mr Sean.'

'Mr Sean, I am the richest man in the history of the world; I am the world first multi-trillionaire.'

'So, Don Pablo.' 'Yes, Mr Sean.'

'In the USA system, one billion is 1,000,000,000 and a trillion is 1,000,000,000,0000, so one trillion is one thousand times one billion, in the UK system one billion is 1,000,000,000,000 and one trillion is 1.000,000,000,000, so one trillion is one million times one billion.'

'I am very impressed with your ability to work that out Mr Sean.' 'Well, Don Pablo, I am good with figures, everybody's good at something.' 'True Mr Sean, very true, he is the richest who is content with the least.'

Don Pablo and Phil were chatting away, and I decided to walk around the plane.

Maria came up behind me, putting her hands over my eyes and saying. 'Guess who?'

'hmmmmm, let me think, I know it's the most beautiful creature who has ever walked the earth, so it has to be you, Maria.'

'Mr Sean, you say all the right things, would you like to share a hot tub with me, Mr Sean.'

Ker-Ching. 'why of course Maria' 'I will go and get my shorts (nobody wears trunks these days).'

(you know the old saying when the tiger pounces, it is going in for the kill, I am the tiger, this is my chance to tell her how I feel about her).

(DON'T F*CK IT UP MR SEAN)

So, I am sitting in the hot tub, nice and warm, then Maria walks in with her dressing gown on, so she undoes the Kelly bow that's holding it together and drops it to the floor, She has no bikini top on. 'I hope it does not bother you, Mr Sean, but I like the hot jets of water to massage my breasts.' *f*cking hell, I can do that for you no problemo.*

No, not at all, Maria, (take deep breaths, Mr Sean).

Wow, what a body, you know by looking at her, she takes good care of herself, she climbs in and snuggles right up to me and starts to kiss me.

'You know something, Maria.' 'know what Mr Sean.'

'Last month, I would have never thought I would be sharing a hot tub with a beautiful girl like you; this is a dream come true for me. I hope it lasts.'

'Why thank you, Mr Sean, you're a very handsome man yourself.

'Yes, I know Maria, it's a bit of a curse, being this good-looking guy, maybe I should have been born a male model.'

'Mr Sean, you have good self-esteem, it's time to have some lunch Mr Sean, can you please hand me my bathrobe?'

Time to show off my body. 'Why Mr Sean, your body is ripped chiselled, and I have never seen a six-pack like yours.'

'Yeah, Maria, I look after my body, I need to have a perfect shape for my work that I do part-time. 'Explain yourself more, Mr Sean.' 'I work as a male dancer, performer for extra money.'

'Why of course Mr Sean and you have a tattoo on your left arm.' 'It's a tattoo of Che Guevara, the best freedom fighter worldwide, the day they murdered Che, they made him a Martyr.'

'Do you have any tattoos, maria?' 'Yes, Mr Sean, I have a shooting star on my perineum.'

'Wow' that's a very tender part of your body.' 'It is Mr Sean' my collage flatmate, and girlfriend, she's a tattoo artist, all of the girls we shared a flat with, we all have a tattoo of a shooting star on our perineum. Ice cubes, and copious amounts of alcohol will freeze anything Mr Sean.

'Maria, may I ask you a question?' 'Why, of course.'

'How long have you known Don Pablo?' 'I first met him when I was 18 years old and started to work for him when I was 20 years old, so it's been 12 years I've known Pablo Escobar.'

'So, why have you never married before Maria?' 'Mr Sean, I have dated some fascinating men, prince's, film actors, etc., etc. and now I am dating a male dancer. I am dating you, Mr Sean.'

You don't have to say that twice, Maria.

Thank you very much, Maria, I was hoping you would say that, but I cannot give you the life you have here with Don Pablo, I am unemployed; I get £54 per week benefit, and work as a male dancer.'

'Please, please, please, Mr Sean, I am richer than your Queen of England.' 'Yes, Maria, but you work, the Royals never did a day's work in their life.'

'Mr Sean, the royal family do a substantial amount of charity.' 'Of course, they do Maria, and the royal family don't do anything else now, do they?'

I can remember Maria the Queen was coming to visit Dundee, to open up some workshop, I remember it, like it was yesterday, a cold September morning. The schools had all the children out waving the Union Jack flags. I was nine years old standing in the cold, in my school shorts. Jack frost was nipping at my legs, and every kid that was there waited 3 hours on the royals, and the Queen drove past the crowds, waving her left hand at the window. It was all over in about 20 seconds, she never even looked at the kids that waited for three hours in the cold. Sorry Maria, all I am saying is that ever since that day, I have never been a big fan of the royals.

I see Mr Sean that one of the royal princes has opted out of royal duties, he and his new wife want to live independently and stand on their own two feet, and to earn a living for themselves. Yes, Maria, but somehow, I can't see Harry flipping burgers at a fast-food chain, or Megs brushing up hair at a hairdresser, they know they can make a lot more money, only because who they are.

Mr Sean, if you had to meet the Queen of Britain right now, how would you act, what would you do Mr Sean?

That's a hard one Maria, I would do what any person that has a connection to Ireland or Scotland, I would shake her hand, but not bow my head, *"and kick her in the pussy" saying fuck your Union Jack we are taking our country back."*

'you are funny, Mr Sean, you make me laugh, Let's not argue about something that does not concern me, Mr Sean, we will take our relationship one step at a time, Mr Sean, do you agree.' (*You better believe it, princess*).

'Why, of course, Maria, so let it be.' 'One more thing, Mr Sean, how can I say you are not that BIG Mr Sean.' 'hmmmmmm, well Maria, a man's genital does shrivel up, and I have been in the jacuzzi for the past 45 minutes.' 'I know Mr Sean; I was only teasing you.'

'Sure Maria, anyway I do have 14 stone to push it in with (*BOOM BOOM*).' 'You are very funny, Mr Sean. 'How long have you known your friend Phil. well, Maria, his dad is a plumber, and he was plumbing in my mum washing machine, that was the first time I met Phil. I must have been about three years old at the time, and we went to the same nursery, primary and secondary school together, so we have been friends all our lives. Phil is not the sharpest knife in the kitchen, Phil used to think a Volcanologist was a long lost relative of Mr spook.'

'I did have you thinking there, Maria, course not, I am only joking with you, Maria. 'Let's have lunch.'

***

'Hey, Mr Sean, how did you get on with Maria, did you pin the tail on her. 'No, Phil, she's not like that, we are taking things one step at a time.'

'So, did you not do anything, Mr Sean? 'yeah, just a wee bit of kissing, and some finger fun, finger fun, yes Phil, finger fun, oh sorry Phil I forgot you think a pussy's got two big eyes and a bushy tail.

'Ha ha ha, Mr Sean, nice one.'

'She is a gorgeous girl, and she has a lovely "chicken madras" (*ASS*).' 'she sure has Phil, and her voice is sexy, ropey broken English accent, I can sleep on a bed made of her voice Phil. 'Yeah, Mr Sean, I would rather be sleeping on her.' 'Hahaha, nice one Phil, but remember don't be talking like that over in Columbia, some people may take offense, it's a different culture.'

'Yes, I know, Mr Sean, you told me.' 'So, Phil, what was Don Pablo saying.' 'He's clever, Mr Sean, he speaks seven languages.' 'It takes me all my time to speak English Phil.' 'Yeah, I know Mr Sean. 'Cheers for that, Phil.

Ha-ha, got you a nice one there, Mr Sean, anyway, speaking to Pablo when you are up close to him look into his eyes.'

Why that Phil.'

Because he wears contact lenses, as do all of his Sicario.'

Well, what's up with that Phil millions of people worldwide wear contact lenses.'

Yes, I know Mr Sean I am, just saying that that's all mate.

'I am only joking with you, Mr Sean.' what you are only joking about Pablo wearing contact lenses.'

No, about you - takes you all your time to speak English; 'Yes, I know, Phil.' one of Don Pablos main hobbies is breeding endangered species. He breeds them and releases them back into the wild. He has his own Safari park back home in Columbia, and the rare ones, he gifts them to safari parks, so poachers don't get them. 'Well, they should not be locked up in zoos or rich people paying money to shoot them. China and Vietnam are the biggest buyers of endangered species, rhino horns, tiger parts, they use them for medicine. 'F*ck, there no need to use animal parts for any medicine.' 'how 'don't they go to the doctor like everyone else?'

Here comes Don Pablo and sex bomb Maria, 'Gentlemen, would you like to order your meals, my chef will make you anything you want.'

'Thank you, Don Pablo, your hospitality goes beyond belief and here comes chef Mario to take the orders.'

'Mr Sean, are you ready to order?' 'Yes.'

'May I have vegetarian ma-po tofu with mushrooms and vegan Chinese noodles on the side followed by vegan banana pudding?'

Phil spoke next with what he wanted. 'Fish, chips and beans followed by sticky toffee pudding, two beers to follow.'

'So, Mr Sean, I am very intrigued to find out how you became a vegetarian, is it for medical reasons or religious reasons.'

'No, not at all Don Pablo, I just like to know that no animals have to suffer for my sake because I need to have some food, that's all Don Pablo, that's all.'

The chef interrupts. 'Don Pablo, would you like to place your order.'

'I will have two lobster served with red potatoes, and mushroom risotto, and a shrimp cocktail as an appetizer followed by a drink of my 100-year-old Scottish whisky.'

'Maria, your order?' 'I will have the same as Mr Sean.'

'Ok, your meals will be served in 15 minutes.'

'Chef Mario.' 'Yes, Phil.' 'Can you skip the two beers; we will have the same as Don Pablo.'

'Yes, if it's ok with Don Pablo.'

'Why, of course, chef Mario, these two gentlemen are my guests.' Pablo responds.

'Chef Mario.' 'Yes, Mr Sean, I was just wondering, how you will cook the lobsters? Boil them like everybody else?'

'Why, of course, Mr Sean, they do not feel any pain whatsoever.'

'I disagree with that Mario; if a living creature has a brain, it will feel the pain, do you not agree with me chef Mario?'

'Well, if you put it in that context, yes, Mr Sean, I do.'

Don Pablo was looking at me, pondering my words.

'Chef Mario.' 'Yes, Don Pablo.'

'Take the lobsters off my menu and inform my hotels and restaurants worldwide, no lobster's to be served from this day forth, also, take lobster off the menu at the banquet I am holding in seven days as a celebration for my birthday in becoming the first trillionaire.'

That's one up for the lobsters.

***

'Compliments to the chefs.' Mr Sean said. 'That was the best meal I have ever had; would you not agree Phil?'

'Yes sure, Don Pablo, it was out of this world, must be good to be rich, eating meals like this every day.'

'It helps Phil.' Don Pablo said, staring at Phil.

I don't think he like that last comment and, neither did his sicarios, and you could feel their eyes burning into the back of our heads.

'It's time to toast, here is to you Don Pablo for your kind hospitality and your generosity, lang may yer lum reek.' *Lang may yer lum reek is an old Scottish saying, which means long may you chimney smoke, this is the best way to wish someone a long and healthy life.*

'And I have never eaten food served on a gold plate, gold cutlery, and your plane is like a 7-star hotel.' 'Thank you, Mr Sean, Phil, excuse me, Maria, Mr Sean, Phil, it's time for my afternoon siesta, we will be landing four hours from now, Maria, please show Mr Sean and Phil to their quarters.

'Phil, pop into my room for a minute, I would like to speak with you.' 'Sure, Mr Sean.

'Here Phil, Don Pablo didn't like that comment about it's good to be rich.' 'I was not thinking Mr Sean.' 'It seemed a good thing to say at the time.' 'Yeah, well, Phil, forget about it, ok.'

'Yeah, so how did you get on with Maria?' 'Well, we are a couple now.' 'Way to go, big boy.'

'Did you pin the tail on her Mr Sean?' 'No, we are taking it easy.' 'I think your virginity is growing back, Mr Sean.' 'F*ck off Phil, hahaha, nice one.' 'Mr Sean, here, I hope there are a lot of girls at Don Pablo's banquet, I can do with having some female company, I've not had a girl in months, my balls are the size of elephants gum-sacks.' *Yeah, you wish Phil, you wish* 'Phil!' 'Yes, Mr Sean.' 'Remember one thing at Don Pablo's Place.' 'And that is Mr Sean?'

'Man discovered fire, but a woman knows how to play with it, don't get your hands burnt, no girl there will even look at you or me, and if they do, they will be trying to make the partner's jealous and all of the ruthless, drug cartels in the Americas will be there. These guys don't fuck around, and I don't want to be chopped up into little pieces and scattered around Don Pablo's animal sanctuary.'

'Yes Mr Sean, I've seen the TV series, chronicling the life, of the Medellin cartel, I am beginning to think, this is a bad idea, maybe we should have stayed home.

'Phil, we are here now, let's make the best of it, two weeks, we will be back home in Dundee, plus we have the rings, sell them and hey presto, we'll have millions of pounds, like winning the lottery, just remember one thing, Phil.

'Yeah, Mr Sean, no hitting on any girls at the banquet, the girls there will only be watching out for their self-interest. They will only be looking for a guy's that's got three and four-figure in their bank account followed by a shit load of zeros.

(MILLIONAIRES AND BILLIONAIRES)

'Ok, Phil!' 'Yeah cool, I've got it.' 'And I will ask Don Pablo who will be at his banquet, I am away to get a beer from the cocktail bar, would you like one as well, Phil?'

'Yeah, sure.' 'Here, Mr Sean, pick up that bottle of 100-year-old whisky and a couple of glasses as well.'

'Phil, we better not drink his whisky.'

'Mr Sean, he's the richest *cunt* in the world, he'll not miss it, and he did say help yourself.

(A cunt is a nickname for a person in Scotland, and only a Scots man can say cunnt with real feeling, it's in the accent).

'Here you go, a nice cool bottle of beer.' I said. 'where's the bottle opener, Mr Sean?' 'Here, I've it here, it's a bottle opener plus a 120 GB memory stick in the handle of it.

'Where did you get that from?' *Phil asked me.*

'Got it from Mr Asiff, from the corner shop, some drink salesman, gave him a few of them, and he gave me one.' 'You got something for nothing from Mr Asiff, was he feeling right?'

Mr Asiff said to me Mr Sean; I have a hilarious laugh today, I switched the push and pull door signs around, on my front doors, watching all they druggie bastards, coming in spending all the money they get from begging. Fecking clowns trying to figure out how to open and close the doors, very funny. I told him they can't help themselves because they are addicted to methadone, heroin, painkillers, it's just like you and all the Asian shop keepers are addicted to making money. Then he said, Mr Sean, to keep one junkie the government has to pay out £40,000 per year for one druggie, they get paid for everything, methadone, taxis everywhere, taxis for their children going to school because the junkies are in their beds too spaced out to walk their children to school, clothes, they even get money for dogs to have as companions, yet I have to work my balls off to make a living Mr Sean, it's is not right I swear to Muhammad, if I were in charge of this Scottish government I'd shoot the junkie bastards.

He's a sad man he spends all day and night in that shop, he tells me, I am up for the roll man, and paper delivery at 6 am. I don't finish till 10 pm, then I go to the back, and fall asleep, then up again at 5.45 am every day. Once a month, I stay at my house at the weekend, my nephews look after shop. He never washes, that's how he always smells of body odour.

And Phil, it is funny when Pablo's sicarios call him boss.

Why that Mr Sean.'

Well, Mr Asiff, says when an Asian shop keeper, calls someone boss, he's calling you an asshole.

That cheeky pakki bastard, he'd always call me boss when I go into his shop'. Here's your paper boss, your rolls boss, is everything going right for you boss?, that cheeky pakki bastard I will give his shop a miss from now on.'

Phil, you never buy rolls from Mr Asiff or any other Asian shopkeeper, Why that Mr Sean.'

Well Phil, the last time I was in Mr Asiff shop I had diarrhoea, and got caught short and had to go to his toilet, but there was no toilet paper, luckily I had some in my back pocket, I pointed this out to Mr Asiff, and he told me Asians don't use toilet paper, they clean their ass with their left hand with Water That's why all Asians eat with their left hand.'

Get tae fuck, Mr Sean, now you tell me, I am never buying rolls from an Asian shopkeeper again.

"That Mr Asiffs, wife, was having an Asian tea party in her garden for all the other Asian girls and one of them said she is going to get teeth implants and a tummy tuck. The other girl said that she was going to get breast implants, so you know how they try and be better than everyone else? the other Asian girl says she's going to get a facelift and a chin tuck, so not to be outdone, that Mrs Asiff turn around and said to them, with a big smile on her face that she is going to get her asshole bleached, the girls look at her in amazement and replied, we can't imagine Mr Asiff with blonde hair.' That's a good one Mr Sean I should have seen that one coming, as the captain of the Titanic said. And another thing, Phil I forgot to tell you, Mr Asiff two nephews' Omar and Muhammad, *The pair Of them dress like some American rap stars, and they wear more gold then MR T,* anyway they asked me if I would sell them my passport.'

Why do they not have passports themselves, Mr Sean?

Course they do Phil, they offered me £500 for my passport because the pair of them are smuggling People into the UK and they would sell on my passport for thousands, to someone who wishes to start a better life for themself in the UK;

How do you know all this, Mr Sean?

Well when I had to go down to Mr Shankley lawyer.' to sign my stripping contract with him, but his lawyer was not available, but the top criminal lawyer in Dundee Mr Russell

Gordon, ushered myself into his office to sign off the paperwork. His secretary phoned him, and he excused himself saying he would be back in five (5) minutes, and there on his office desk was a file-folder,' with the names of Omar and Muhammad on the file. I had a look-see,' do you remember the case a few years back in Dundee, about the two prostitutes, K L Rennie and Fiona Campsmell, they used to pick up the clients from the Marketgait in Dundee?

Yes course in do Mr Sean,' they were working with that rogue DR L.E. Moffats, he used to give them Drugs for the two prostitutes, to knock out the unsuspecting clients, and take indecent photographs of the men, and DR L.E. Moffats had the two prostitutes take photographs of himself, performing a sex act on them, and blackmailing them in a flat in the housing scheme in Beachwood. That place is the ghetto of Dundee,(*I remember driving through Beachwood, with my windows up of course, at 2 am, and a little kid about four (4) years old was standing on the street corner smoking a joint, I rolled down the window, just a little, and said hey kid you shouldn't be out here at this time it's freezing, he replied course I should man, man's got to live, you want to buy any drugs? If not feck off or I will put a brick through your car windows. I shouted out the window, get it right up you, you little fecking prick, I'm just trying to help you. The other day I was driving through Beechwood, at about 3 am and got a flat tyre, so I had to get out and change it, this place is unsafe for anybody at 3 am even the police don't go here after midnight. If they must, they are with an armed response unit. That's how bad Beechwood is it's a fucking ghetto, so I am changing the tyre and this girl - a heroin addict about 23-year-old. Still, she looked like she was 55 years old, total mess, hair untidy, her face all spots and her lips covered in cold sores, says hey pal I need some drugs man I have not been high for three hours. I'll suck your dick for £15 pal, I replied no fecking way, look at the state of you, you have not washed in weeks, you have not changed your clothes in two to three months, feck that I will give you £2).*

"That's a cheap joke - if it wasn't for the grace of God; it could be you or I."

Well, the pair of them are out of jail now, and they are working with Omar and Muhammad, they are running the brothels in Dundee.'

Ok, Mr Sean, but what has happened to DR L.E. Moffats.'

He's still in jail, he got ten years for his crimes, and he got gang-raped from seven (7) guys in prison,'and K L Rennie and Fiona Campsmell got five years. Mr Shankley my boss, sorry old boss, tipped off the police about Omar and Muhammad, and he told me the pair of them are into every money-making scheme you can think of. From drugs to running brothels, they get girls from the EU, very good looking ones, offering them good jobs here in the UK. Once the girls are over here, they take their passports off them and put them to work in the brothels, And they're into people smuggling as well and also they are in protection rackets, Asian shopkeepers, night clubs, you name it, and they will be taking money from the owners,

Put it this way Phil, how many 21-year-olds do you know you drive a Lamborghini Aventador worth £250.000, You don't get one of these cars from short-changing customers in your uncles shop! All you have to do is to take a look on social media, their photos with the car splattered on their Social media pages and I don't think they are that clever.

Why that Mr Sean?

Because the police also check out other people on it, that's how the police get most of the information - from the people themselves, Phil.'

And I think Mr Asiff is in it as well, that's how I am surprised that he gave this to me.

'Yes, I know he never gives anything away, and it fits right on my key ring, after we have had the beers, I am going to lay down for a couple of hours.'

'Yeah, Mr Sean, I am going to crash out too for a while, but first …'

I suddenly cut in. 'Phil, I've been looking on the internet using my mobile phone and reading about the Columbian drug cartels, they make the WAFFEN-SS look like alter-boys.'

'Tell me more then Mr Sean.' 'Well, if you cross them, fuck with them, they shoot you, but if you piss them off, they kidnap you and torture you for days, they cut off your fingers, all of them, then cut off your toes, your ears, then your fucking lips and then, they skin your legs alive, they even cut off your eyelids, so you can't close your fucking eyes. And there's a doctor there with them, he pumps you full of that adrenaline shit, he inject it right into your heart with a big needle, so you don't pass out or die, you can do this up to four times, in five days, then if you're really lucky, they spray petrol on you, then they light you on fire.'

'You're a right cheery bastard, aren't you, Mr Sean? Have you ever thought about becoming a holiday rep for the Columbian tourist board?'

'All I am saying is watch yourself Phil.' 'Ok will do big boy.' 'Phil, stop calling me big boy.'

Speaking about the WAFFEN- SS Phil, do you know who the Sonderkommando where?

Sonder, sonder, sonderkommando yeah course I do mate, remember we did a project at school about World War Two, when we were in the final year. They were Nazi prisoners made to work emptying the gas chambers victims of the Holocaust, why do you ask that Mr Sean?

You impress me, Phil, I thought you would have forgotten about that, with all that weed you've been smoking.'

No way it does not matter how much weed I smoke, I can ever forget about that, the pictures are embedded in my subconscious, why?

I had just remembered Phil while I was down at the vet's with Notch this older man came in with his grandson, and his grandson was about 50 years old. This old guy started to talk to me as we were waiting because some emergency came in. He was telling me he was in the Nazi death camp In Treblinka in Poland because this guy was 16 years old and he was 6'7 tall he was given the job as a Sonderkommando. This man called Klass, says he had to watch as the prisoners were made to line up while going in to the gas chambers. This evil prison guard called Ivan the terrible, even though these people were going to their death, this Ivan used to beat the people while they were in line. I mean this bastard was inhumane, he cut off woman's breasts, cut off men's testicles, he'd repeatedly stab them, poke out their eyes, with his very own hands he had killed thousands of people. Tens of thousands more when he was the gas chamber operator. He says Ivans time came when the prisoners rebelled and killed him in his bed in the Treblinka death camp in 1943.

I saw a documentary about that on flix-net a couple of days ago. A Ukrainian man working in a car factory in America, was accused by the American of being the notorious SS guard Ivan the terrible and of course Israel asked for his extradition. So he was made to leave America to stand trial, as Ivan the terrible. In the trial after the Russia army liberated the camp, former SS death camp guards signed a letter saying Ivan mnartach Jenko was, in fact, Ivan the terrible, but after they signed the statement, the Russian army shot them. After seven years in Israel, John Demjanjuk, was found not guilty of being the sadistic guard in the extermination camp and put back on a plane to the USA. Still, the American government continued to go after him as an SS guard, and deported him to Germany where he was found guilty of being an SS guard and crimes against humanity and jail for five years, but died in a retirement home waiting for his appeal to start.

"Ivan the terrible was afoot soldier to the Nazi genocide."

'Here Mr Sean, that Pablo is mega-rich, he's a lucky man, Pablo's that lucky, he will wake up dead one day and find out what's he's died off and rectify the problem that kills him before he goes to sleep that night, *Work that one out.'*

'Yeah Phil, but you know what they say, "don't be envious of evil people and don't try to make friends with them"' the Olmec cartel is the most powerful organization in the world, Pablo Escobar is the most powerful narco trafficker in the world he's head over 60 cartels in the Americas alone, and head of 300 cartels worldwide, the Mexican Drug traffickers, smuggler, and dealers, pay homage to Jesus Malverde "angel of the poor" "the narco-saint" for protection, he's the patron saint, now they pay homage to Pablo Escobar, as do all the drug cartels world-wide.

'Now you say that Mr Sean, we are in the devil's pit now mate.'

THREE HOURS LATER

'This is captain Larsson speaking, we will be descending, and ATA will be 20 minutes.'

'Time to buckle up the seat belts.' 'Big boy.' Phil screams into my ear.

'Don't be calling me a big boy over at Don Pablo's place.'

'Why, Mr Sean, because the people there will think we are buffy boys.'

'It's only a bit of fun Mr Sean.' 'I know, I know, but just knock it on the head, Phil.'

'Cool, will do Mr Sean, will do.'

'This is captain Larson; we will be landing at Jose Maria, Cordova international airport in Medellin in four-minute. Don Pablo, I hope you had a pleasant flight?'

What an arse licker, he knows who pays his wages.

Fuck, look at everybody on the runway waiting for Don Pablo to welcome him back, half the bloody army and the police force is out there and all the high ranking Colombian officials are in the suits, there will be congress, senate, and the house of Representatives, and most of them are waving the Columbian national flag, they treat him like a king. Well, he is the *king of cocaine.*

'Here, Mr Sean, have you noticed that all the customs and security are smiling at you and me?'

'Yeah, don't worry about it, they are just polite.' 'That Don Pablo must be wealthy, his photo is everywhere at the airport.' 'Well, he does run the whole of Columbia and employs hundreds and thousands of people here in Columbia, we will have to get our passports stamped.'

'Please, gentlemen, this way.' Said Mahmoud, Pablo, and Maria have gone ahead of the pair of you, and he will see you at his residency.

'That's good, Mahmoud.'

'And I will be escorting yourself and Phil to Don Pablo's mansion.'

'Mahmoud.' 'Yes, Mr Sean.' 'That's some plane Don Pablo has.'

'Yes, Mr Sean, you will be surprised when you see his mansion.' 'Well, I can imagine.

'The top architects designed Mr Sean, Phil, his house from around the world, the price tag for Don Pablo's super mansion was 357 million dollars, it boasts of ....158 bedrooms.........all with en- suite, it has five underground levels, level 1 is the gym, sauna, hot tubs, Olympic size swimming pool, and tennis courts. Level 2 houses Don Pablo's Antiquities collections from around the world, it's the size of two American football pitches.

Level 3 contains Don Pablo's classic cars, every classic car you can imagine, Don Pablo owns it.

Level 4 houses Don Pablo's amusement centre, Level 5 is Don Pablo's rest area.'

Pablo has 400 kilometres of roads to travel around his estate, and he also has three landing strips not to mention the 13 man-made lakes, and countless condominiums scattered around the grounds; 'He sure knows how to enjoy himself, Mahmoud.'

As we were drive through the countryside. 'Mahmoud.' 'Yes, Mr Sean.

'Can you tell me what is behind the brick wall that we have been passing for the last 20 minutes, and who are the guys with the machine guns, lining the road?'

'Mr Sean, behind the wall, is Don Pablo residency and the men are sicarios, they are here to guard Don Pablo and his family, the wall surrounds Don Pablo property, the wall is 13 feet high and is 13 feet thick, all 25 miles of it.'

'That is some size of ground Mahmoud.' 'Yes, Mr Sean.

'It has four man-made lakes where his pink flamingo lives, all 400 of them, he has a safari park which has lions, tigers, elephants, gorilla's, hippos, in fact, any living animal that lives, Don Pablo will have it there in his safari-parks. The park alone has 300 park ranger and keepers tending to the animals, Pablo also has a man-made 50-foot waterfall, built in the side of the hill, at the rear of him mansion', there is a corridor leading to a door, behind the door is a room that is at the back of the waterfall, Pablo will sit there for hours at a time, he says the sound of the waterfall, helps him to relax.

Yes, Mahmoud, I have been told that the sound of a waterfall helps people to relax, anyway, 'Mahmoud, why did Pablo build his walls 13 feet high and 13 thick?'

'Mr Sean, 13 is Pablo's lucky number.'

'I take it Pablo's not superstitious, not in the slightest.' 'Mr Sean, not in the slightest, he will no doubt tell you why 13 is his lucky number, Pablo like to tell everybody new that he meets.

***

Upon entering the mansion, we were greeted and ushered in by Pablo himself.

'Welcome, welcome, welcome, Mr Sean, Phil, I would like to introduce you to my family, here is the most beautiful woman in the world, my wife, Natalia.

'Please to meet you, Natalia.'

'Here is my eldest Luciana, she is 21 years old, and my second eldest Sofia, she's 19 years and the princess of the family, Camilla, she is 12 years old.'

Just then three, dogs came running around the corner of the mega-mansion, sprinting at full speed up the marble steps, through the massive doors barking all the time, happy to see their master Pablo, 'I do not have any sons, but here are my boys, my dogs, the big white boxer is called Max, the black one is called Ben, and last but no means least is called Satanta, Max was a gift from Blackie, he got him from his sister, who's boxer Sheba had pups, Ben was found by myself while, Natalia and myself where coming back from our honeymoon in Hawaii, he was found injured lying at the side of the road, teenagers were throwing stone at him, I ordered my motorcade to stop, and I pick up Ben from the side of the road, the rain was lashing down at this time, and put him beside myself and Natalia in the back seat of the Bentley Continental GT, my top veterinary surgeons fixed ben's back hind bone it was shattered into many pieces the operation was very successful, but the surgeons said that he would never be able to run again, and as you can see he is now 100% fit, now Satanta, was a gift from father Mackie, he'd had brought him back from Ireland as a gift, I believe Satanta came from an old lady that father Mackie, Holy cross church, Diocese in Kerry, father Mackie named him Satanta, is another for Cu' Chulainn a great Irish Warrior.'

Yes, Pablo, I had heard my dad talking about Satanta/Cuchulainn; from tails, he used to tell me when I was young, Pablo, my I ask you a question?

Yes, of course, you can, Mr Sean.'

The boys that where throwing stones at Ben at the side of the road, what happened to them?

I had my Sicarios to kneecap them to teach them a lesson, I think the next time they come across an injured animal, that they will help it, once they can walk again, my dogs are everything to me Mr Sean/Phil, they are house dogs, they are members of the family, they do have the run of the house and of course the gardens, they also have kennels at the west wing of the house, just in case the weather is hot, the kennels do have air conditioning, and the dogs have their very own pool, they also have their chef.

'Welcome to our home Mr Sean, Phil.'

'I have never seen such a luxurious house anywhere in the world. Don Pablo and your house are breath taking.'

May I ask Don Pablo, why is there a church on the grounds of your garden?

Mr Sean Phil, it is a replica of St Patrick cathedral, my grandpapa two times removed worked And died, along with four other Colombian immigrants constructing this magnificent building; I had my Architects build this replica of this magnificent cathedral, as a tribute to them, It sure is a lovely neo-gothic style roman catholic cathedral and it a great tribute to them Don Pablo; 'Thank you Mr Sean, myself and Natalia are the only people that have been married here, in this cathedral this is where father Mackie blessed the pair as one, you will meet father Mackie soon; Sorry for the interruption, Pablo, but I read somewhere yourself and Natalia were married in Hawaii.'

Yes, this is correct Mr Sean, but Father Mackie insisted on repeating the wedding service here in the cathedral; it's one of many hundreds of buildings I have here in Columbia. I have thousands worldwide, but this is my primary home here in Columbia, the butlers and maids will take you to the individual guest quarters, we will be having lunch in one-hour time, enjoy your stay here.

As we were showing to the guest quarters. 'Here, Mr Sean.

'Yes, Phil.' 'Don Pablo's wife is so good looking.' 'Yeah, you don't have to tell me that twice.

'And she looks as young as her two eldest daughters, do you think she has had plastic surgery?

Either that Phil or Pablo has found the mythical fountain of youth.

And his two older daughters are first-class honey.

'Yeah, Phil keep your eyes off them, remember what Mahmoud said, these are Don Pablo's girls, keep your hands and eyes off them.'

'I know, I know, I know.' Said Phil.

And remember Phil, do you think Pablo became the wealthiest person in the world by trusting every person he meets?

course, not Mr Sean, so what's your point?

Think about it Phil', all the rooms in the guestrooms will be bugged, so watch what you are saying, Phil; ok will do big boy; Phil knock that on the head, calling me big boy.

Sure, think Mr Sean.

'Here is your room, Mr Sean, Phil, if you need anything, please dial 0 on the phone and someone will come and attend to your needs. *Said the Butler.*

'Thank you very much, butler.' 'Please call me Chico, Mr Sean, Phil.' 'ok, Chico will do.

Four-poster beds, gold toilets, jacuzzi, this is the life; not even the best hotels in the world offer this to their guest.

'Can't wait to see the rest of the house.' 'Yeah, I know Mr Sean, the grounds of the house must be some sight.'

'We better have a shower to freshen up before lunch with Don Pablo and his family.'

Later, we met with Don Pablo.

'Well, Don Pablo, that was a sumptuous feast.

'Mr Sean, that was lunch, the banquet will be sumptuous.

'Don Pablo, are all the toilets in your super mansion made of gold or only in the special guest quarters?'

'Yes, Mr Sean, and my family's toilets.' 'one more thing that got my attention, Don Pablo.' 'Yes.

'I thought that a person with all your money, there's not many, how can I say it, nice looking cars parked outside your house.'

'Mr Sean, Phil, all of my cars are in the underground garage, and I have hundreds of classic cars after we have tea in the gardens, I will show you and Phil my car collection.'

'Thank you very much, Don Pablo, we will be looking forward to viewing your cars.

***

As we made our way to the gardens. 'Hey Phil, have you noticed all the steps and stairs are marble?' 'Yes, Mr Sean and even the Corinthian columns at the front of his house are marble.'

'Please sit here, gentlemen, Don Pablo will be in your presence in a minute or two.'

Mr Sean when we get home, I've been thinking about spending the money I get from selling the ring I would like to make and sell my own after-shave with the money, and I am going to call it *"The pussy catcher,"* what you think about that, Mr Sean?

At least you are getting creative, but calling your aftershave *pussy catcher*, I don't think many girls will buy their partners a bottle of aftershave called the *pussy catcher*, mate.'

The aftershave is targeting the single guy, not couples, *big boy*, after all, that's what single guy's think about all the time, is it not Mr Sean?, and I was thinking about bringing out an aftershave for bisexual men called *"any hole will do."*

I can see it now, Phil, and I will be the first to buy two bottles from you ok mate.

Sure, thing Mr Sean, you will be the first person to get two bottles of *"any hole will do."*

Very funny Phil, you should call an aftershave after you *"Cannae get pussy."*

Here comes the main man now with blackie, his sicario.

'Sorry to keep the pair of you waiting, Mr Sean, Phil, we needed to perform due diligence in investigating yourself and Phil your criminal records, Mr Sean, Phil, we have run your fingerprints through the international criminal police organization more commonly known as Interpol.'

'Ok, Don Pablo, how did you get our fingerprints?' 'Mr Sean, Phil, from the glasses when you were having your meals.' 'ok, why did you not ask for them?'

'Mr Sean, you were charged with shoplifting one bottle of whiskey, you receive a fined of £50, fixed penalty.' 'Yes, that was a long time ago.'

'Don Pablo ...' 'Please do not interrupt me, Mr Sean.' 'Phil, you were charged with stealing women underwear from a washing line.'

'Yeah, Don Pablo, let me explain, I did it for a dare back home in Dundee, it is called snow-dropping, but

unfortunately, a woman saw me and reported it to the police.'
'Strange customs over there in Dundee, Phil.'

'Yes, Don Pablo, the things you do when you are young.'
'Young Phil, it happened two years ago!'

'Here, Don Pablo, I don't think it is fair that you are checking into our background like that.

'Please, Mr Sean, Phil, I had to be sure who I was inviting into my home, for all I knew, you could be DEA drug enforcement agents.'

'Yeah sure, how many DEA agents do you know that speak with a Scottish accent at this time.'

Don Pablo and blackie are having a good laugh at the two of us.

'Well, Don Pablo, I've have been checking you out as well before we came here, you are the head of Olmec drug cartel, you supply 85% of the world cocaine to mainly the USA, and you supply all of the other drug cartels in the Americas with cocaine, and you launder all the money through your company.'

'Mr Sean, 85% is that all? I was thinking I was supplying 99% of the cocaine to the world, and you forgot to say that the Mexican cartel that works for me supply methamphetamine to the USA as well to every cartel in the Americas work for me; next time, please have your due diligence up to date. I have no competitors in the narco business because everybody works for me, Mr Sean.'

'Yes, Don Pablo, you have also built thousands of homes for the people who live in poverty.'

'Mr Sean, no person in Columbia, lives in poverty now, that was one of my goals to rid poverty out of Columbia, to take from the rich and give back to the poor.'

I will tell you this Mr Sean; a Colombian peasant farmer; earned \$20' in the '90s for working six days per week, the farmer, his wife, and all the children worked the land from 8 am to 7 pm;

Now fast-forward to the year 2020; the same farmer works for myself, he earns \$250 per week working 8 am to 5 pm four days per week, his wife is now at home' the children are at school getting educated; Where they will gain scholarships for college'. I have 1 million farmers working for myself Mr Sean, Phil.

'Yes Don Pablo, you have also built, hospitals, schools, colleges, free health care for the needy, free education for everyone, you have also created thousands of jobs, you have pulled Columbia out of the dark ages into the present. *If only every government did that for the poor, the world would be a better place.*

'I have Mr Sean, indeed, let's have tea and then we will go to my underground car park.

As we were walking back to the super mansion. 'Don Pablo, I must say you like your marble.'

'Yes, Mr Sean, every room in my house has marble flooring, it's very cool to the touch, marble is a metamorphic rock composed of recrystallized craniate minerals, all of the marble the top Architects used comes from Italy.'

'Also, the chandeliers in the main hall are the biggest I have ever seen.

'Mr Sean, these chandeliers are made of the most delicate crystals money can buy and the rarest Crystals in the world, all sixteen of them, at the entrance to my home.

'Tell me Don Pablo, for having the world's biggest collection classic car; you must have excellent security.'

'We have Mr Sean, the perimeter wall is 25 miles, that surrounds my home, sicarios stand 300 yards apart.'

'So, Don Pablo, you have 150 of your scenarios outside the wall?'

'Yes, Mr Sean, I also have 500 sicarios inside the walls, I have the most sophisticated security in the world, CCTV cameras everywhere, microphone every 100 yards, pressure pads buried in the gardens, apart from the safari-parks, drones keep an eye over the parks, and the gardens. Apart from my bodyguards (sicarios), I also have hundreds of people operating the cameras and security of my property.

'You must have an awesome collection of cars Don Pablo.'

'Mr Sean, I do and wait until you have seen my collection of Antiquities from around the world, Mr Sean, I have more Antiquities than any of the museums in the world put together.'

***

As we continued to walk, I probed more into Don Pablo's life.

'So, Don Pablo, where did it all start for you?'

'Mr Sean, there is a myth here in Columbia that Pablo Escobar buried most of his money and killed the people that buried it, that is not true, he was making $60 million per week, it all started for him in 1975, within a matter of months, he was making $60 million per week until 1993 when he came to an ugly end on December 2nd, 1993 when he was tracked down and murdered by American trained police and military forces.

He had a team of experts including myself, we invested $ billions and billions in everything, banks, property, hotels, car manufacturing, airplanes, etc., etc., right under the noses of the Columbian government.

Now, as you know, I am the world's biggest cocaine kingpin in the world, and the wealthiest person to have ever walked the earth.

I am the world's first Trillionaire. I make one billion dollars every week (*that's some wage packet*)'

'How do you manage to move all of the cocaine Don Pablo?'

'Mr Sean, you are asking too many questions, please stop now, I would not want to have my sicarios take care of you, Mr Sean. *Fuck, that's a bit heavy.*

'Your wish is my command, Don Pablo.'

'Good, let's keep it like that, Mr Sean, Phil.'

'Don Pablo, I've never asked you anything.' *Said Phil.*

'I know Phil, but I am telling you too, I am a businessman.' Don Pablo replies to me and Phil.

'Yes, Don Pablo, we know you are?'

'I provide a service to the people, just like any other business, I am going to point out 3 points for you, 1, 480,000 deaths are caused each year in America due to tobacco.

2, 88,000 alcohol death each year in America.

3, 22,000 lives are lost due to drug abuse in the USA alone; around 4,000 death is the direct result of cocaine indulgence.

So, that leaves 18,000 deaths, which are due to prescription drugs made by the pharmaceutical company; they all pay taxes to the American government, and nothing is said to them. Now, I don't pay taxes to the USA, and that is an itch under their skin, if the USA taxes cocaine, then nothing would be said, that's only the deaths in America. Worldwide, millions of people die each year due to alcohol, tobacco, and pharmaceutical drugs; they are uncountable.'

"In the first three months the world health Organisation, says it's a new highly addictive cocaine that's been flooding every town, every city in the world as we know it, it is a significant problem the

World Faces Fifty-six thousand babies were born addicted to cocaine worldwide in the first two months of 2020".

'You see Mr Sean, Phil, the biggest killers in the USA and the world are alcohol, tobacco, and pharmaceutical industry, do you see where I am going with this?'

'Yes, Don Pablo.' 'My business is a grain of sand on the beach compared to all the people that died at the hands of the Alcohol, tobacco, and pharmaceutical companies, in 2020, more people died of opioids painkillers overdose in American than was killed in the Vietnam war, no doubt these companies had to give a large amount of money to Donald trumpet presidential campaign.

Ebola virus is eating its way through Guinea in Africa, as well as the rest of Africa, now 16,000 people have lost their lives due to Ebola in Africa, yet two American doctors working in Guinea contracted Ebola, now these doctors were flowing back to American and put in quarantine and giving "a magic pills", within one month the doctors now cured of Ebola are now living a healthy life again in the USA,

Yet people are still dying in Africa, Guinea is a big experimental laboratory for the pharmaceutical companies they have the cure for Ebola, but because Guinea is a third world country the leader can't afford to buy the pills, it's like black life does not matter, it's all comes down to one thing Mr Sean, Phil, money, money make the world go round, I am not a rich person, I am a poor person with money, Mr Sean, Phil.

'I am just a small coch in the mechanics of business, Mr Sean, Phil, worldwide millions of people die every year due to these company's operations everybody has their chemical addiction; Mr Sean, be it alcohol, tobacco, drugs, the Olmec cartel is a business.'

As we went through the automatic doors, anybody else would have used stairs going down to the underground garage, no, but Don Pablo had lifts he has them all over his house.

'Please, Mr Sean, Phil. After you Blackie, can you press number 3, please?

'Yeah, sure thing, boss.

Blackie was a big guy, 6, 5 inches tall, muscular body frame, a scar on his left cheek, black hair, tanned complexion.

As the doors open at floor 3, amazing sight lay before myself and Phil, we have never seen so many classic cars in one place before, hundreds of them, from E type Jaguars, Maserati's, Auston Martins, Mercedes gull wings, Boss Mustang, Corvette Stingray, Ferrari Dino, Lamborghini's,

Bugatti's, every classic car you can think of, Don Pablo had it he even had his private race track where he can drive his cars for enjoyment. They say money can't buy happiness, but it can buy everything else, lucky bastard.

"What was it Pablo said again, too win the lottery you have to work to buy the winning ticket, Mr Sean/Phil, yeah sure I can just see Pablo, going to a cash machine getting his on-screen balance, you have $ FIVE TRILLION DOLLARS, the maximum you can take out is $300 today, it's just not going to happen is it big boy"

'Don Pablo.' 'Yes, Mr Sean.'

'This old car that has holes in it; it does not appear to be a Classic car.'

'Mr Sean, this car once belongs to Bonnie Elizabeth Parker and Clyde Chestnut Barrow, aka "Bonnie and Clyde." In early 1934, Bonnie and Clyde stole this V8 for and drove it around the Midwest robbing banks and killing people, the joyride ended when lawmen punctured the car (and Bonnie and Clyde) with over 234 bullets, this 1961 Ferrari 250 GT California SWB spider cost me $27 million, 1954 Mercedes Benz W196 silver arrow, price tag, a mere $45 million, the list goes on Mr Sean, Phil, if I had to put a price on my collection, it would be more than $ 1-3 BILLION, give or take a few hundred million. Tomorrow, I will let you take my cars out onto the test – track.'

I quickly responded. 'This is a dream come to true Don Pablo, how can we ever pay you?'

'With respect, Mr Sean, Phil, with respect, now I am feeling jet-lagged, please forgive me, it's 10 pm, I will have to retire for the night.'

'10 pm! We have been down here looking at your classic cars collection for three hours, and please forgive Phil and I for keeping you so long.'

'The butlers will wake you in the morning for breakfast, good night, gentlemen.'

'Good night, Don Pablo, Blackie. Thank you very much.' 'Till morning, gentlemen.'

'Here, Phil, before you go to your bed, pop in my room for a chat.' 'Yeah, ok, big boy.

'Phil, stop calling me big boy.' 'I am only joking Mr Sean.'

In my room, we had a chat. 'Here that's some collection of classic cars that Pablo Escobar has, he has more money than most of the small countries in the world.'

'Yeah, and he knows how to enjoy it.'

'Mr Sean, did you smell blackie breath, it was stinking of garlic.' yes I sure did, a lot of people eat garlic, they say it's good for you, and do you think it was wise to tell Pablo Escobar that we knew he was a drug kingpin?'

'Yes, he knew we would have had checked him out on the internet.'

'Yeah, I also check out his wife, she's an Eastern-European, top supermodel, they married 21 years ago, Pablo Escobar hired an island in Hawaii, he took over all the hotels there, even took over all the helicopters so that nobody can take any photos of him and the bride and of course, all of his guests; they say the price tag was only a few million dollars, a small change to him.'

'Would you not agree, Phil?' 'Sure, Mr Sean, Pablo Escobar is such a cool guy, he does remind me of that guy who played the P.I, even the way he talks and acts, he would pass off as his brother, yes and his daughters got the looks of their mum, eastern European with olive skin, I wonder if they follow in their mother's footsteps.'

'No way, the girl's will not want for anything, Phil, anything.'

'Yes, I know Mr Sean, and they say crime does not pay.' 'Nobody has told Pablo crime does not pay, he's the happiest man I have ever seen, I have been thinking Mr Sean, can I ask you a question remember when we were in London in the hotel, and Danny dyers were there with his daughter.'

Yes, course I do Phil; it was only a few weeks ago, mate.'

And you say Danny dyers is a pricks, prick, well Mr Sean what is a pricks, prick?

Phil, let say Mr Asiff is a prick everybody knows, that right?

Yes, Mr Sean, he's a first-class prick.'

Well, Mr Asiff would call Danny dyers a prick, so that makes him a pricks, prick you see?

Yes mate, I got it now.

Later, in the day Mr Sean, do you still have the sunglasses I gave you?

I do Phil, and they are in my suitcase why?

I was walking around the grounds at the west wing, watching Pablo's dogs playing in the pool with other dogs, and Blackie was about 10 feet behind me, and it was like he snarled his teeth at me, and they were fangs, massive big fang-like teeth, he never knew I had on these mirror glasses.'

Phil, maybe it was just the sunlight catching the mirrors glasses at a different angle.

I am not too sure about that, Mr Sean.

'Mr Sean, breakfast will be served at 9 am, 1 hour from now downstairs.'

'Thank you very much, Chico, Phil, and I will be there at 9 am sharp.'

Morning Phil, did you have a good night's sleep?

Yes, I sure did, Mr Sean; how about you, big boy?

Phil stop calling me big boy. Sure Mr Sean' well, did you have a good night?

Did you not hear the wolves howling then Phil?

I never heard a thing Mr Sean; I was sound asleep,

Something strange happen in the early hours of this morning' Phil I woke up about 5.30 am and made a coffee, from the coffee maker in my room, and opened the patio doors and was standing on the balcony', there was a foggy dew, swirling about the gardens, there was no full moon, but the stars were shining bright.'

Hold it, Mr Sean Here comes Chico.

Right, Phil, I will tell you after, but I can guarantee what I am going to say to you will freak you right out, mate.

I can see it in your face, Mr Sean, whatever happen freaked you out as well.

It sure did Phil, and I am going to ask Pablo about the wolves and the other strange noise I heard as well.

Tell me then Mr Sean?

Gentlemen, please, never keep Pablo waiting, it's is very impolite, don't make Pablo angry, the pair of you would not like to see Pablo angry.

Yes, chico, we will be right there, here Phil that chico should chill-axe.

Later in the dinner room, Don Pablo and his family walked into the room 'Good morning Mr Sean, Phil.'

'Morning Don Pablo, Natalia, Luciana, Sofia and Camilla.'

'Did you have a good night's sleep?' *Don Pablo asked.*

'Yes, I have never slept in a four-poster bed before, it was very pleasant, and my room has a hot tub, sauna, and steam room, your house is like the most significant eight (8) star hotel in the world don Pablo.

'Thank you, Mr Sean, it's only the guest rooms that have the extras, all 159 of them.

'Don Pablo, I woke early at about 5 am as I went out to the balcony the foggy dew was swirling around the grounds, it was very humid.'

Mr Sean, this is Colombia, it has a very different climate to Scotland.

Yes, of course, Pablo.

please continue Mr Sean.'

as I was saying' while sitting on the balcony' I heard maybe about 100 yards from me wolves howling and dogs barking' Mr Sean you must be mistaken there is no record of any wolves in Colombia; Pablo, it was definitely a wolf I know a wolf howling when I hear it as I used to work in the local zoo doing volunteering work with wolves.'

Please, Mr Sean, as I said before, there are no wolves here in Colombia. Still, I have an ancient Inca drinking vessel' in my collection of Antiquities' there is a legend and a story to it, you will find very interesting, another one of my hobbies is Archology, I have paid the Peruvian Government $ 3 billion, for myself and my Archaeologists, and scientists, to spend one month at Machu Picchu, where we will have total Access; good can't wait to hear the story, and Pablo one more thing, can you tell me about all the vans coming up the driveway.'

'It's the pyrotechnics company for the celebrations in two days, Mr Sean, and I am sure I have told you this before.'

'Yes, Don Pablo, please excuse my ignorance, the last couple of days have been mind-blowing for myself and Phil.'

'Phil does not talk much, does he, Mr Sean?

'No, Don Pablo, he was dropped on his tongue when he was a child.

'Hahaha............ I like you, Mr Sean, you have some humorous sayings.'

'Phil's Ok; it takes time for him to come out of his shell Don Pablo. So, Don Pablo, who is on the guestlist for the celebration party?'

'ALL of Columbian government will be in attendance, also, my business partners, (drug cartels) and people that I have been close to over the years, actors, sportsmen and women, politicians, etc., etc., etc. After breakfast, I would like to show you and Phil my collection of antiques from around the world.'

A little bit later, I and Phil, Don Pablo, and a man named Scorpion went down to view Don Pablo collections. 'Scorpion, please press level three.'

Scorpion is one of Don Pablo's sicarios, mean-looking guy pothole face, very dark eyes, he does not look at you, he stares through you, he stands about 5,10 tall.

'As you wish boss, the room was just like his car garage, massive, and the first collection here is Ancient art that was stole in Mexico, 350 priceless objects from the Mayan, Aztec Inca civilization.'

'I believe that they were taking on Christmas day 1985 and then you got them on the black market, Don Pablo.

'No Mr Sean, they were given to me by the Mexican Cartel, as a, how would you say, a gift for my business, here the drinking vessel I was telling you about it was found in a cave some years ago with these two stone table with Egyptian hieroglyphics the story goes.' *two hours later*, Pablo, how very interesting.'

these paintings are from the best in the world, Leonardo da Vinci, Vincent van Gogh, Rembrandt, Caravaggio, Raphael, these are some of the most priceless works of art ever painted.

'fuck, no way is that the fucking Mona Lisa painted by Leonardo da Vinci in 1503?'

'Yes, it is Mr Sean, the very one, but is that not in the Louvre Paris, the one in the Louvre is not genuine.' 'So, it's a fake, Don Pablo.

Everywhere you looked there was a masterpiece, nobody on the outside world can comprehend the masterpieces here, hundreds if not thousands of them.

'Yes, it's a fake Mr Sean, Phil.' 'But Don Pablo, most of these paintings are priceless.

'So, they say Mr Sean, but one thing to remember is nothing is priceless, everything has a price, a man who has nothing has no price, Mr Sean.'

'Right, ok then Don Pablo, so how much money did you pay for the Mona Lisa.

'Well, in 1965, the painting was insured for $100.000.000, I paid $ 1 billion for her, and £ billions more for every antique here, Mr Sean, just as a past time.'

'You are not going to tell me that this is the face mask of Tutankhamun, Egyptian.'

'Pharaoh of the 18TH dynasty, it is the very one, Mr Sean, on infidical bases, you have a good knowledge of history?' Mr Sean?

'Yes Pablo, history was my favourite subject, when I should have been at school, I was in the library reading history books.

'So, did someone just walk into the Egyptian Museum in Cairo and walk out with it?'

'No Mr Sean, it was taken from the museum during the Arab Spring uprising, 'The uprising started in Tunisia, by a fruit seller, protesting about taxes he had to pay to the government, he was a courageous man. On December 18th, 2010, and then sold to the highest bidder, myself, I out bided everyone else; I can't remember the final price $ 1-3 billion, I believe, but I will return them all to the country and to the people from where they were taking from 'well done Don Pablo.' 'it is the least I can do, Mr Sean, Phil, I do not know when this will happen, but it will happen one day.'

'Don't tell me Pablo but are those china's emperor's Warriors.'

'Yes, Mr Sean, I have 20 figures of them, and I suppose you got them on the black market as well, Pablo.'

'No Mr Sean, these are gifts from China, a thank you gift, for me employing more than 1 million of their people, I also have the world's most significant collection of prehistoric dinosaurs I have four hundred full skeletons and fossils in the room, please follow me, gentlemen, *everywhere you looked was skeletons*, this one here is the largest herbivorous specimen is

Titanosaurs Argentinosaurus Huinculensis, this creature here is scelidosaurus, to the left this one is Dilophosaurus it is or should I say it was a meat-eater, this one is the biggest of them all Prosauropods a leaf-eater, this stego, and Triceratops and he was found in American, this was the most vicious dinosaur, and the most famous one T-REX Tyrannosaurus, the hight of the T-REX was 4.8m-6.9m tall, Mr Sean what do you call a baby T-REX,?

Well, Pablo I would probably call it sir'......

As I said before Mr Sean you have a facetiousness sense of humour, the other one here is Diplodocus, and Brachiosaurus, and Brontosaurus, these where massive dinosaurs, the bigger they were, the better chance of survival they had, every prehistoric creature that has ever walked the earth, I have seen them alive with my own eyes, maybe I can take you there some time? *"Two hours later."*

'It will soon be lunchtime, let's go and have lunch.'

'Your collection of antiques and Dinosaurs are out of this world Don Pablo.'

'Feel free to come down here anytime, Mr Sean.'

'Thank you; I can spend days down here looking at your Antiquities.'

'I am happy you like my collection, and you are more than welcome.'

THE LESS YOU BELIEVE THE MORE YOU HAVE TO FEAR

Pablo was doing my head in talking about their fecking dinosaurs, Mr Sean; he knows more information about Dinosaurs than a palaeontologist does, what they eat, their mating habits, how many hatchlings they have.

Phil, Pablo did say that he has seen the dinosaurs up close in the flesh, do you remember him saying that?

Sorry mate, I am that stoned, I was trying to figure out what way the earth is spinning mate.'

Phil people that smoke that shit, think about a load of shit mate, I see it in your eyes they are knocking together Phil, let us go and have a walk around Pablo's grounds.

I have an app on my mobile phone it tells you about all the riches people in the world how much money they have and what they buy, listen to this Phil, some Saudi Arabian prince has preliminary valuation of the state's oil company as $1.6 TN, and three of the biggest oil companies in the world had joined forces to buy it, and Pablo bought it for $1.7TN, and Pablo's collection of his classic cars and all his properties world-wide are worth more Than the head of Amazon Jeff burrito, and the wizard of computers Bill gates, and Facebook owner, Mark sucker fucker, put together, you are talking $billions.'

You got it wrong mate, the head of Amazon is Jeff Bezos, and the head of Facebook is Mark Zuckerberg, so that's the second, third, and fourth wealthiest people in the world, that is some going ah.

Mr Sean did you believe that story Pablo, was saying about, the *werewolves* and man-size *vampires*; Phil, Pablo's hypothesis explains so many facts.

(K) Mr Sean.'

Let talk over by the waterfall, Phil, stand here next to the falls, no mic will pick up anything we say, Too right I believe him, as I was saying before, I was standing on the balcony drinking my coffee, I heard Pablo dogs barking, it was just like play barking', any dog would do when playing around, Then I listened to the wolves howling, maybe four or five of the howling, and a swishing and Screeching Sound like, well, like a big bat would make, just like Pablo said.

No way, Mr Sean, has Pablo put you up to this to try and scare me, mate.

Phil, this is the truth, mate.'

I am getting worried now, Mr Sean, but go on, tell me more.

So I am standing looking out into the foggy dew, and I see maybe six or nine man-size figures, Plus you had the dogs as well, all of a sudden the figures all turned and stared right at me, I froze, their red and green eyes were, burning through me, like looking saying I should not be there the figures all started to run in my direction, the sound of their feet hitting the ground was, Like in time with my heart beating, the main werewolf jumped from the ground to my balcony, Had to be about 25 feet high, it was massive, not like the werewolf you see on the films; it was like a more up to date werewolf, like a demon-like werewolf, big hairy beast with massive fang like teeth, and pointed ears like a wolf, a man-wolf and beside the werewolf was a bat the size of a man, it had two legs, two arms man-size body with the head of a bat wings everything it was a human body that had morph into a bat and all of the walked upright just like a man, Both of them had Teeth about four inches long, they were about 3 inches away from my face, I snapped my eyes close as the impact was imminent, and nothing happened. I open my eye the sun was rising over the hilltops, and in the distance, I saw Pablo's sicarios walking away into the foggy dew, laughing with Pablo's dogs and the main werewolf that jumped at me was smelling of garlic.

Blackie was smelling of garlic, Mr Sean.

You have hit it on the head mate, blackie and the rest of Pablo's sicarios, were the *werewolves* and the *vampires*; Fucking hell, Mr Sean, but there was no full moon.'

Yes, I know Phil maybe they have evolved through time, remember Pablo said, they came from a fireball.

Yes, Mr Sean.

Well what if that fireball was their spaceship, crash landing on earth about 5oo years ago, then Pablo has brought them back into the 21st century, by drinking virgin's blood from the vessel, he did say, he who drank virgins blood from the vessel who one day rule the world, and he does rule the world he's the world's number one cocaine supplier.'

Yes, Mr Sean and Pablo did say, he bought the vessel from an old archaeologist, that found it in a sealed cave near Machu Picchu in Peru, along with three skeletons, one skeleton had an Inca high priest headrest along with two other bodies, the wolfman, and the bat-man; which today are knowing as the *werewolves and vampires,* the two Egyptian hieroglyphs tablets.'

Yes, Phil, but what are two Egyptian hieroglyphs tablets doing here thousands of miles away from Egypt, I have taken some photos of the tablet's front and back, and a video of the drinking vessel.

What's the point of that, Mr Sean, you can't read the hieroglyphs?'

Yeah, I ken Phil, but once we get back home, I will get a book out of the library about hieroglyphs and with sometimes be able to decipher it.'

Ok So Mr Sean the Inca, sacrificed children to the gods for a better world and or during a famine they sacrificed virgin children as they were the purest of humans to the *werewolves* and the *vampire,* To stop them from killing all the Inca people, The Inca people did sacrifice children to the gods, but two years later they did, sacrificed them to the Ancient Aliens, *werewolves, and vampires.*

'Well way to go sherlock, did you think of that all by yourself, Phil?

I don't know Mr Sean, it all just came to me, like someone was talking through me.

You must have picked up the vibes from the vessel; the children must have been talking through you Phil, this is getting spooky, it is like something out of the Twilight Zone, Yes, Mr Sean, but the lust for blood was so great for the *werewolves* and the *vampire,* that somehow the high priest tricked, the pair of the bloodthirsty *Ancient Aliens,* into the cave, where the priest was. Still, unbeknown to the pair, the Inca men were outside and sealed the cave with the three of them inside never to see daylight again, the hight priest Villac Umu, gave his own life to save his people, but 18 years after the event, the Spanish came and looted all the treasures, of the Inca and killed the people in the year of 1532.

It's mind-bending Phil, and I bet you anything that Pablo drank virgins blood from the vessel, and that how he's now the wealthiest person in the world, he must have total control over the *werewolves* and *vampires*, he's had that vessel for years, all of his other drug cartels must be like his sicarios, all Ancient Aliens these monsters are all over the world, you never know Phil, they may be like *freemason* what do you mean by that, Mr Sean?

Well, Phil, they say your never ten feet away from one of those bastards.

I am going to go back down and pick up the vessel to see if I can get any readings from it, Mr Sean.

Right Phil I, will me you back here in say ten minutes?

Sure, Mr Sean, *fifteen minutes later.*

Mr Sean, I never got much feedback from the vessel, but their spaceship never crashed here on earth It is still here, and it is under Machu Picchu in Peru, the Ancient Aliens, helped the Inca civilization to build, Machu Picchu, with their vast knowledge there are thousands time more Technologically Advanced than humans; also the *werewolves* and *vampire* can move anything using *Telekinesis, it's simply the ability to move an object without coming into physical contact with it* so with their superpowers it took them and the Inca people three weeks to build it, but without the Ancient Aliens it would have been years in the making.'

That right Phil, because the Inca people started to build Machu Picchu, in the year, 1450 Pablo said, Then without warning the *werewolves and vampire, began* to attack the Inca people for blood, Because they need blood like humans need food.'

Ok, Phil, so why did they end up in the cave?

An albino child was born, the Inca high priest, told the Ancient Aliens, that the child was a gift from the gods to them, and the child had to be sacrificed in the dark, so that how they ended up in the cave and one more thing Mr Sean, there was a lot of gold in the cave as well; the old archaeologist must have taken all the gold, I would have taking the gold myself, Mr Sean.'

Right, now I see Phil everything is coming together like a jig-saw puzzle, but there was no child body found in the cave, and Pablo must know something about the spacecraft, under Machu Picchu! And the gold must drain the Ancient Aliens, off their power, that's why they could not escape from the cave Phil, watch out here comes Lucianna.

"Killing is as easy as breathing to all of Pablo's sicarios"

'Phil, Mr Sean,' 'Yes, Lucianna.'

I want to show you and Mr Sean my Dancing horses; you know "Dressage" is a highly skilled form of riding, performed in exhibitions, competition, as well an " art pursued solely for the sake of Dancing with horses.'

'We never knew that Luciana, it will be a pleasure to watch you perform with your horses, 'After lunch, then?' 'Of course, Luciana.

'Mr Sean, it is bad manners to be using your cell phone at the breakfast table.'

'Sorry, Pablo, I am trying to post a message on social media, to say that we have arrived safely.'

'Mr Sean, you said not to tell anyone that we were coming out to Columbia.'

'Yes, I know Phil, I posted that we were going to Benidorm in Spain, so chill out Phil.'

'ok, Mr Sean.'

'Sorry Don Pablo, as I was saying, I am trying to post a message on social media.'

'Yes, yes, yes, Mr Sean, I know.'

'Maria, can you take Mr Sean to your office and let him use your computer?'

'Why, of course, Don Pablo, after breakfast.'

'Phil, I will catch up with you and Luciana at the Dressage horses.'

'Maria, shall we?'

As we walked into the lift, a person came in as well, Pablo Escobar sicarios, he was well trimmed, I think he's a bit of a poser.

Please follow me Mr Sean as we walked into Maria's office. 'Please, Mr Sean, I will set up the computer.

'There you go Mr Sean, and it is all set up for you to use, I will give you some privacy, would you like a drink?' 'Coffee, please, Maria.'

'I will have to go down and get you one, Mr Sean; I will be back in 5 minutes.'

'Looking forward to seeing your beautiful smile, Maria.'

***

'These horses dance so gracefully, Lucianna.'

'The world's best Dressage trainers train them, Mr Sean, Phil, these horses are all from the bloodline of Arabian horses, they are the best dressage horse money can buy, these are very valuable Dressage horses, excuse me, it's time for their feed.'

'I would like to see them again soon. Lucianna, thank you very much.'

'You are more than welcome, Phil.'

'See you soon, Lucianna, one more thing Lucianna, can I ask you a question?' 'Yes, of course, Phil, who are the Chinese men watching over you?'

'These are my bodyguards; they are Shaolin monks, my father brought them over for me because I do not like guns, they are with me all the time, especially if I have to go outside.'

'ok then, see you later.' Phil said.

Phil and I turned away and started walking back to our room. 'Hey Phil, don't even think about it.

'Think about what Mr Sean.' 'Yeah, you and "Lucianna," you know what I am saying, Phil.

Later in our room. 'Ok, Mr Sean, be cool, so did you post on social media.'

'Yes, and I downloaded everything that was on Maria's computer. I put it on my memory stick.'

'Why did you do that, Mr Sean?' 'Just felt like doing it, that all, don't tell anyone Phil, ok?'

'Yeah, sure.'

I later went downstairs to a massive sitting room where I met Pablo relaxing. 'Mr Sean, is everything good for you now?' 'Yes, Pablo, thank you very much. I could not help but notice a picture of you shaking hands with someone on Maria's desk.'

'Yes Mr Sean, his name is Santiago, Santiago is in charge of the Mexican side of my empire, everybody calls Santiago the Mexican, You will meet him the day after tomorrow, he will be here as all of the Americas cartels.'

***

'Hey Phil, there is a photo of Pablo shaking hands with a guy called Santiago in Maria office, and I have checked him out on my mobile phone, and he's the head of the Mexican cartel.

'So, your phones working now, Mr Sean?'

'Yes, it is but wait till you have heard this, his drug cartel stormed a drug rehabilitation centre in the north of Mexico and killed 88 people who were trying to get off methamphetamine, the police report says that all the bodies are mutilated beyond belief like a pack of wild animals, had attack them that's how evil these fuckers are, and they stop at nothing; as do all the drug cartels in the Americas, they all do it under the wings of Pablo Escobar. That cunt, Escobar thinks he's a living god, he has the power over life and death, if he says a person dies, that person will be dead that very day.

***

'I think we better call it a day and tell Pablo that there is an emergence back home, and we will have to leave asap, what do you think of that Phil?'

'Yes, let's wait till after the party, after that, we can tell Pablo that we have to go home in 48 hours, we can be on a plane out of here.' 'ok, Phil.'

'We will plant the seed and tell Pablo that one of your family members has been in a car crash with a serious head injury.'

Having this in mind, we went to search for Pablo in the huge mansion and found him talking with one of his sicarios; I quickly broke down the bad news to him.

'Why Mr Sean, Phil, this is terrible news, I will arrange for Maria to book your tickets right away so you can be at the bedside of your family member.' 'Thank you, Don Pablo, my brother will appreciate your kindness.' 'We are getting updated on social media all the time, Pablo, he's in a stable condition just now, so we will stay and catch the flight home after your celebrations on Saturday But if his health deteriorates, I will tell you asap Pablo.

'Phil, I have booked tickets for you and Mr Sean, traveling on Monday noon, you will be back home in under 15 hours.'

'Thank you very much, this is very much appreciated, Maria' 'If for any reason you have to leave sooner, please tell me, and Pablo will use his plane.

'Very kind of you and of Pablo Escobar.'

As Phil walked away, I tapped him on the shoulder. 'Here Phil, that was a good bit of acting, you should get an Oscar for that.'

'Yeah, cheers, Mr Sean, all I want to do is get to feck out of here and be back home.

'Soon, Phil soon.'

'I am away to go to see Lucianna at the horses.' 'Ok Phil, I will catch up with you, later, I would like to check out more of Pablo's Antiquities collection.'

As I was walking around the collections, there was a door at the back, as I opened it, there were display cabinets full of shrunken heads, very eerie feeling came over me, some of the shrunken heads were very old, yet some, only a few weeks old.

'Mr Sean.' 'Fuck Pablo, I just about jumped out of my skin.' 'Sorry to startle you, Mr Sean, but you are not permitted to be in here.' 'So sorry Pablo,'

'There is a notice on the door saying no unauthorized person permitted.' 'Oh, sorry, Pablo, but I don't read or speak the Spanish tongue.

'That's good, Mr Sean, but I read somewhere that Spanish was compulsory in schools in Britain. ' Well, not in Scotland Pablo, the most Ambitious person in my class at school wanted to be a train driver, but we all told him "nooooooooooooooooooooooo000000 way" will you be able to drive a train, We all told him, the people at this school shine the shoes of the people getting on the train, that's how weak Scotland Education system is Pablo.'

It's bra' working in the big hoose, so it is.

'Is this one of your jokes, Mr Sean?' 'no Pablo "it's a fact" when I should have been at school, I used to be in the library reading history books, that's how I acquire a good knowledge of history.

'Can you tell me Pablo about the shrunken heads in the cabinets.'

'Mr Sean these are my unique collection, I have always been fascinated about shrunken heads for many *years, head-hunting* has been practiced in the north western region of the Amazon rainforest by the tribes that stay there, they are the Jivaroan, Shuar, Achcar, Huambisa and the Aguaruna tribes. Most countries outlawed selling the heads in the 1920s, and head shrinking was banned worldwide, by the 1960s. I have kept the tradition alive, about 95% of the people in the cabinets are my enemies, people that have double-crossed me, political figures, fellow drug cartel members, judges, police, member of the search-block that murdered Pablo all those years ago, there are over 800 people in the cabinets, this is the newcomer to my collection. Look, Mr Sean closely, you have seen him before. Yes, that's the manager from your nightclub in London.

'Tony Rogers.

'That is correct, Mr Sean.' 'Why do that to him, Pablo?'

'Mr Rogers stole four diamonds from the watch you handed over to him Mr Sean, he stole from me, I noticed the diamonds were missing as soon as he gave the watch back to me Mr Sean, he confessed to my sicarios after some persuading.' *This Pablo's off his fucking head.*

'Everybody has a magic number Mr Sean; if a man has a mouth, he has to eat Mr Sean, a man will do anything for money, I am going to make you an offer Mr Sean, please consider it very carefully, I will give you £7 million of your British pounds if you take this gun and shoot Phil through the heart.

'I am very sorry, Pablo, but I will have to decline your offer.'

'Mr Sean, £13 million, that's my final offer.'

'No Pablo, I will not do it, he's is the closest friend I have, I have known Phil since we were at school together, I cannot and will not do it, Pablo!'

'Mr Sean, you are a real friend to Phil. I will not ask again Mr Sean, and I was looking forward to adding Phil to my collection.' *I better not tell Phil about the heads and what Pablo asked me to do.*

'Mr Sean, do you know why the shrunken heads mouth and eyes are sewing close?'

'No, Pablo.'

'They do that to trap the soul of the person; then the warriors tie the heads around there waists to put fear into the other tribes, then after one year, they discarded them; once the

Europeans came and discovered them, murder became wholesale, hundreds of people were murdered to satisfied the western world morbid fascination for shrunken heads.' *Is he for real, he's the one that's got a morbid fascination for shrunken heads?*

'Pablo, I never knew that thank you for enlightening me on the culture of the Amazon head-hunters.' *The quicker Phil and I get out of here, the better, this cunt, Pablo off his fecking head, and I've got a feeling that we may end up in his collection of shrunken heads.*

'You see Mr Sean, I have to be 13 steps ahead of everybody in my line of business, *"you ken what I'm saying there big-boy."*'

'You have been listening to myself and Phil talking, Pablo, have you?'

'As I said Mr Sean, I have to be 13 steps ahead of everybody Mr Sean.'

'Mr Sean, I have heard everything you and Phil been saying, Phil is very disrespectful, what was it he said about Natalia, *"she's fecking honey I'll love to spit-roast her and smash feck out "o" his two daughters."*'

'Don Pablo, I am very sorry, Phil was just talking in the Scottish street talk, he was just saying how beautiful your wife and daughters are.' *'Change the subject, Mr Sean.*

'Pablo, forgive me for the asking, but why is the number 13 lucky for you, your wall surrounding your super mansion is 13 feet high, and the walls are 13 feet thick, etc., etc., etc.'

'Mr Sean, I was born on Friday the 13th, I met my beautiful wife Natalia at a fashion show in Milan on Friday the 13th, I am voted into the Congress of Columbia and the Senate on Friday the 13th and to add to the facts Mr Sean, once voted into the Senate, I usurp the house of representatives, my political party "E.P.P." are in total control of the government with 156 seat out of 172 seats.

'Pablo, what does E.P.P. stand for?' 'Of course, Mr Sean, "Escobar People Party."

Not so long ago, Mr Sean, Columbia was ruled by a wealthy family, money was everything to these people, they never bothered about the poor, Columbia was one of the most unstable countries in the world, there were countless murders every day here in Columbia, I made a vow to rid corruption out of the Senate and most of all, out of Columbia.

'You do hold the people of Columbia very close to your heart Don Pablo.

'Thank you, Mr Sean.' I come from a poor background, my father had to scour the rubbish trash looking for anything to resell when I was born, and I always said when I became rich, no man would ever have to do that to survive to put food on the table for his family.'

'Can I ask you Pablo, how much are you worth, being the richest man in the world?'

'Mr Sean, you are not a rich person if you can count your money!'

'Well, Pablo, I get £80 per fortnight from the government in Unemployment benefit.

'You forgot to say the money you get from dancing or should I say stripping.'

'Mr Sean, Maria did say you are a male dancer.' 'Pablo, I get paid about £60 per night, about twice a week.' 'That is excellent Mr Sean.' So, Pablo, are you going to tell me how much you are worth?' 'You ask too many questions, Mr Sean, as I said before you are not a rich man if you can count your money Mr Sean but I am worth between £two to three trillion of your British pounds, $five trillion.

I have more money than most countries in the world Mr Sean.'

(As they would say in Dundee Scotland, he's a lucky bastard).

Phil and I decided to have some relax in front of an Olympic swimming pool inside the mansion. 'Saturday morning, this time next week, we will be back home in Bonnie Dundee.

'Yeah, Mr Sean, can't wait for it.'

Pablo's voice suddenly interrupts our thoughts. 'Mr Sean, Phil.' 'Yes, Pablo.

'All of my guests will be arriving at 6 pm, but my cartel friends will be here at12 am, I would like you to meet them.' 'Of course, Pablo, it will be my pleasure to meet your business associates.'

'But first, I would like to show you and Phil my special animal reservation.'

'The helicopter will be leaving in 30 minutes for the short journey, and you will see the most amazing animals you will ever see in your life.'

After 5 minutes, we were in the back of Pablo jeep driving through the mountainous terrain.

As the jeep came to a standstill, Pablo handed me and Phil binoculars.

'Have a look over there, between the trees, gentlemen.'

In the opening was a group of Gorillas.

'These Gorillas are the most endangered species in the world, and they are called the cross-river Gorillas, the leader of the troop is the white one (albino), he's called Kong, he's king around here, I saved him from hunters who had killed his mother and father and the rest of his troop, I hand-reared him myself. The hunters that killed Kong troop, and all the top hunters in the world, were all invited over to my home for a hunting expedition, the prize was $15,000,000,000, but the hunters became the hunted, all of them were dropped off at one of my animals sanctuary with no guns, if they made it to the boundary walls, they would all be giving $15,000,000,000, but no one came out alive.

I watched the animals hunting the hunters on my closed-circuit TV; there is nothing like seeing a "paper men" crumble with fear, Mr Sean, I have rhinos, wolfs, hippos, lions, **cheater,** I have a group of south China tigers, they have not been sighted in the wild for more than 30 years, all of my animals have been breed by my scientists and researchers from around the world, they have cloned Amur leopards, Pteronura brasilliensis, Javan rhinoceros, red panda's, Tasmanian devil, white and black rhinoceros, Hawaiian seals, Iberian lynx, Malayan tigers, Sumatran Elephant, every endangered spice have been cloned.

'Well done, Pablo, you are a credit to the wildlife, if only other countries can follow your way of thinking about saving the endangered spices for this planet.

'Thank you, Mr Sean, my animals, are shipped around the world to safari parks, so people can see them, to see what animal came close to being extinct forever, my scientists are very close to a breakthrough in growing human organs, a breakthrough is imminent, Mr Sean months not years, nobody will have to wait for organ transplants; all organs will be grown in a laboratory, from that person's stem-cells so the recipient will not have to take drugs for the rest of their lives because the body will not reject the organs. After all, it's growing from their own stem-cell. It's not playing God, Mr Sean, it's giving life to the needy. Pharmaceutical companies will not be happy because they make $ billions every year providing drugs for the body not to reject the donor organs, that's why the practice is banned around the world, not because it's unethical, but because pharmaceutical companies will lose money, they have spent $ billion around the world, giving monies to political figures to stop the practice, getting the go-ahead, as I said before money make the world go around. It's time to make our way back for my guests will be arriving.'

***

'Here come all the cartels with their entourage coming up the drive and by helicopters, the first to arrive was the Mexican Santiago.

'Don Pablo, you are looking well.' 'Thank you, Santiago, and you have lost some weight, Santiago.'

'Only on the shoulders, Pablo, only on the shoulders.'

'Natalia, you are looking incredibly beautiful.' 'Why thank you, Santiago.'

'where are your children?' Santiago asked.

'You will meet them later on Santiago, this is Mr Sean, and his friend Phil, they are from Dundee Scotland UK, these are the men who handed in my lost watch, I was telling you about Santiago.

'Please to meet you, Mr Sean, Phil, any friend of Pablo's is a friend of mine.' 'Thank you very much, Santiago.'

'Let's talk in private Santiago.' 'Why, of course, Pablo.'

After the two hardcore had moved away from us. 'Hey Phil, that Santiago is a mean-looking bastard, and so is his sicarios.'

After about an hour later.

'Please, Mr Sean, Phil, join Santiago and me for some refreshments.'

'So, Pablo, how big is your animal reservation.' 'Well, Mr Sean, It's 50,000 square yards.

'So, Pablo, its nearly 29 square miles.' 'That is correct Mr Sean; you have a good ability to work that out so fast, hasn't he, Santiago?'

'As I said before, Don Pablo, I am good with figures.' 'Yes, so I have seen Mr Sean.

'I have been watching you look at my wife and daughter; *Now, three things can happen here.*

1. *Go head to head with Kong, and I don't fancy his chances.*
2. *Get dropped off in the middle of the animal sanctuary, and we all know what happened to the hunters.*
3. *Wing it.'*

'*Bullshit my way out of it, think I'll go with number 3, I am good at bullshitting,* Don Pablo, your wife, and daughters are like oil paintings, their beauty should only be admired from afar.'

Pablo walks over to me and puts his hand behind my neck and whispers. 'You are like the son I always wanted; you are welcome to this family Mr Sean, always.' *Nice one Mr Sean, it was squeaky bum time, i.e., shitting myself.*

'You are more than welcome, Pablo, more than welcome.

'Some of the Mexican scenarios were giving Phil a hard time calling him Geronimo referring to his American Indian looks.'

'Phil, ignore them, Geronimo was a great Indian warrior, 'Here, Geronimo is Mr Sean, your female squaw, they, Mexicans are a bunch of pricks.'

'Here, I have a question for you, Mexicano.'

'Yes, Mr Sean.' 'Well, what the difference between a spider and a Mexican?'

'I don't know Mr Sean; well you have more chance of getting a spider in the bath than a Mexican.'

All of Don Pablo's sicarios were laughing at the Mexicans, Antonio, the mouthpiece of the Mexicans, was not happy saying, "I get you, you Gringo bastard."'

'Yeah, only in a re-run, Antonio. You fucking prick.'

'Now-now, men we are all family here, no ill-feeling toward one another.' Pablo says.

'Sure, Pablo, just a bit of light fun.'

The leading Mexican sicario is called Antonio, Bernardo, Carlos, Chago, Dacio, Humberto, Honorato, they all looked like a bunch of Mexican bandits from the "1800's", very untidy, put it this way, a scarecrow has better dress sense than them. Still, apart from Pablo, they were wealthy all of Americas drug cartels were very wealthy, and they are all here, all 40 of the world's head drug cartels plus their sicarios as well, each top guys had six sicarios with them, all meaner than the next!

'Mr Sean, Phil.' 'Yes, Pablo.'

'The banquet will start at 8 pm, 8 hours from now, and it is tuxedo's that all males will be wearing, my tailors will here in 15 minutes, they will make yourself and Phil your tuxedo in under two hours.

Three hours later.

'How does your tuxedo fit, Mr Sean, Phil?'

'Very well Pablo, they fit like a glove, as we say back home in Dundee Pablo.

'Good, my tailors are the best in the world, Mr Sean.'

***

Banquet time 'Why Maria, you look out of this world in your red dress.'

'Thank you very much, Mr Sean, and may I say, you look like a Scottish secret agent in your Tuxedo Mr Sean.'

'Yeshhhh, Miss funny fanny, well, we do share the same name.' 'You're so funny, Mr Sean.'

'Would you like this dance, Maria?'

'You dance well to Columbian music, Mr Sean.' 'Well Maria, this music is going next on my soundtrack when I am doing my stripping.' 'Well, Mr Sean, you will never have to do that again, not when I am here with you, once the firework starts, come with me.

Everybody are all standing out on the lawn, all 2,000 guest and the display kicks off, it was like all the new year's party worldwide, all rolled into one, and at the end, there was a giant Effigy of the main man himself Don Pablo.

Escobar, holding the head of the US president, Donald trumpet, all thirty feet of him.

By this time, Maria was taking me by the hand, down to Pablo's garage, she whispers in my ear.

'I want you inside of me.' As she opened the back door of this big American classic car, *I saw a gun.*

'Maria, why is there's a gun under the passenger seat?'

'Mr Sean, Columbia men always keep their gun under the passenger seat, come lie down with me.'

Here we go, Dundee, man on tour. As she lay on the back seat, her legs parting every second. 'Come, Mr Sean lay down beside me.'

So, I did as any Dundee laddie do, pounced on her like a Tiger going in for the kill, hand right up the kilt (skirt).

'*ooooohhhh*, Mr Sean, you know how to use your hands.' She said as she bit her bottom lip. 'Don't stop, *that's sooo goooood.*'

'Mr Sean.' *Her breathing is getting heavy now, and my ears are burning with her hot breath.* 'Ooooooooo, Mr Sean, take off your ring, it's uncomfortable.'

'Maria, that not my ring. It's my watch.' 'Excuse me, how dare you! I have never been so insulted in all my life.' *She smacked her cell phone off my eyebrow causing an old cut to re-open, and blood started to pour from the old war-wound, by the time all of this was happening,* Maria was in the lift, going back to the party and I was trying to stem the flow of blood from my opened wound.

As I was in the lift, I must have pressed any button to find a toilet, once the elevator stopped, I darted out and opened the first door I came upon, there on a pool table was a naked girl, about 20 years old with these two older gentlemen, snorting cocaine off her naked body and in the corner, two older men giving two younger girls a *"Columbian snowstorm."*

'Hello Mr Sean, come here and try some of Columbia finest cocaine, have a line or two.'

'No thank you, gentlemen, I am looking for a toilet.' 'There is one here, Mr Sean.'

Before I even got to the toilet door, one of the men said. 'Come, Mr Sean have a line, it will do you no harm.' 'Well.' I said. 'I have to disagree with you there, because of long term abuse, taking that shit causes long term psychosis severe depression, cardiac arrest, widespread ischaemic vascular disease, stroke, Seizures, Respiratory arrest, and cocaine Psychosis, *AND THEN DEATH.*

'Are you a doctor, Mr Sean?' 'No not at all, I am a doctor of life.' 'Keep off the shit because one day it will fuck you up and all those around you it may cause a mental illness, or it may not, but some people are born with a mental illness; it may lie dormant for year then all of a sudden it appears not only affecting the person but all around them as well it's a disease like cancer, one of the biggest killers of all time, nobody asks to catch cancer it just happens, just like a mental illness.

I left the place in a rush to find Maria and ran into Phil. 'Fuck sake man, I am going to have to see Maria, I am going to have to apologize.' 'Hey, Mr Sean, where have you been?' 'I have been looking for you all over the place.'

'Sorry, Phil, but have you seen Maria?' 'I saw her about 10 minutes ago, heading outside Mr Sean, is everything ok?'

'Yes sure, Phil, I just must see her, that's all Phil.'

Mr Sean, I was having a long talk with blackie, and he was telling me that he's 72 years old.'

No way Phil blackie is about the same age as Pablo, say about 45 years old, not unless blackie has the Reversal of Benjamin Button Disease.'

Blackie asked me a funny question; he said if you were a cartoon character, who would you like to be?

That's a strange question, Phil, well what did you say?

I told him I would like to be Daffy Duck "*Woo Hoo Hoo, and they'll never catch this little duck*" that was his favourite saying, Daffy Duck's cool as Mr Sean.'

Why not Pepe Le Pew, because you never get the girls.

Ha, ha-ha, tell me when to stop laughing, mate, who would you like to be then?

Aye, dinnae ken Phil, will have to think about it mate and tell you later, ok mate.

'This place is full of A-Listers celebrities, look there Mr Sean, it's the big man, *Arnie, "I'll be back, "I vont your clothes your shoes and your motorbike."*'

'Arnie never said that he did say I'll be back, and he never said I vont your clothes, your shoes, and your motorbike.'

' He fecking did so Mr Sean, in the Terminator when he came through the wormhole back in time, when he is walking into that bikers cafe, he said it to the big biker, remember, and the biker stumped out his joint, onto his chest !'

'ok Phil, I remember, and it was not a joint, it was a cigar, Phil.' 'Yeah, that's right Mr Sean and look who's Arnie's talking too, that other great actor Al Pacino; remember him in that film when he was just starting his acting career, are you talking to me, remember when he's looking in the mirror, are you talking to me.'

'Phil, it was not Al Pacino that said that it was Robert De Niro, that was in that film called, I forget it mate, but it will come back to me, Al Pacino's was in that film about the Cuban immigrant called Tony Montana, and he's saying in the movie was "say hello to my little friend."'

'You know the saying, Phil; you say it every time you go to the toilet.' 'Cheers, Mr Sean.'

'I am only joking Phil, and I am going now to find Maria.'

'Phil your eyes are all glazed, have you been smoking some of that Columbia Rastafarian, marijuana?'

'Yes, I had a wee cheeky smoke with Lucianna.'

'Are you off your fucking head Phil, if Pablo finds out you've been smoking grass with his daughter, he will cut off your fecking balls man, keep away from her, Phil ok, there are lots of girls here, it's like walking into the Playboys mansion, you can have your pick of all the singles girls here, but keep away from Pablo's daughters, for feck sake what are you thinking about, sometimes I worry about you, Phil.

'Will do Mr Sean and good luck finding Maria, there are hundreds of people here.'

'Cheers Phil, but first look over there, it's that guy that played the part of *William Wallace*, "freedom," I have to shake that man hand, it's funny, but at school, no books or the teachers said anything about William Wallace, it was like the English government tried to eradicate him from Scottish history, it was not until he made his film about *William Wallace* that many people know what had happened to him and Scotland is still being repressed by the English government, Scotland will not be free until she has her second referendum for independence. But even then, the English government has sucked all the oil out of the north sea, and to tell you the truth, Scotland should have voted for independence forty years ago and would have been one of the most prosperous country's in the world, the reason I say the English government is because it's the English people that votes in the new government, the Scottish, and welsh people do have a say. Still, the people in England do have the casting vote, Phil, I have read about

William Wallace, the time he spent in Dundee, it all kicked off in *the year 1291 when Wallace was completing his education in Dundee in a church school run by William Medford, the vicar of Dundee.*

That year the English king, Edward 1, seized control of Scotland and installed English governors into every Scottish castle, including the castle of Dundee, a few months after that, William Wallace got into an argument with the English governors son, Wallace ends up stabbing the guy to death, that was the first blow for Scottish independence against the English, and we all know the story of what happened, with the fight against the English, now fast forward to the present day, the church in Dundee, ST Paul's it's on the high street, stand on the site where the original castle used to be, has a plaque commemorating William Wallace time in Dundee Sunk into the wall of the church, so what did the English government do? They put a big statue of Admiral Duncan, to honour him for the victory of the battle of Camperdown 1797, they could have put the statue any were in Dundee, but no, they had to put it in front of the plaque of William Wallace.

And imagine Scotland votes for independence Scott's will be recognized as an official language How hard is that going to be to learn, can you imagine a group of Chinese tourists, talking Scottish And Going it to a chip shop and saying,eh'll hae twa peh's un a poke o chips an, an ingin ane an ah.", or I'll, gie ya a skelpit lug! Haud yer wheesht loon, we'll hay tae skedaddle aff f'it like loon is yer h'unds cald, it's just not going to sound right someone else from a different country trying to talk Scottish, but one thing good will come out of it, a lot of Scottish people will get jobs teaching Scott's all over the world, or maybe hire Scottish people to translate scots into English.

'It's like you on your soapbox again, Mr Sean.'

'Think about what I have just said Phil, it's true, remember when Mel made the film about the last 12 hours of Jesus Christ before he was crucified, the film industry shunned him because the Jews were not happy about how they were being portrayed in the film.

"Even when Judas hanged himself there was a storm too"

'Mr Sean, it was the Jewish people that crucified Jesus, they had the choice to crucified Jesus or Barnabas, and they voted to let Barnabas go, that is the history of how it all happened, so why are they trying to re-write history?'

'That's right Phil, and I will tell you another bit of history, the man that gave the people a choice, "Pontius Pilate" served under Emperor Tiberius, Pontius Pilate was born in Perthshire in Scotland!'

So that's why Scotland has shit weather them.

'And if only the world superpowers complain to Israel about the treatment of the Palestinians in the west bank, as much as the Jewish community complains about his film, the world would be a better place, well over there, it would be, eh Mr Sean?'

'Yes, I know Phil, but that would never happen because all the superpowers are selling Israel weapons costing "billions of dollars a year."'

'Look at all the people around Pablo Escobar, most of the people think Pablo lives off unicorn liver pate" he's just a streetwise down to earth guy.'

'Yeah, Mr Sean, you forgot to say he's the richest man in the world, that's how he commands respect everywhere he goes.'

'Anyway, Phil, I have to go, I have just seen Maria, '*Hasta la vista baby, I'll be back.*'

There she is, out on the lawn, it's funny there are hundreds of people around, and she stands out like a beautiful woman that she is.

'Maria, look, I was only joking, it's just a saying back home, you know I would never, disrespect you in any way, shape, or form, I am truly sorry, I will never say that again, I do apologize with all of my heart.'

'Mr Sean, your men, treat women like meat, do not say anything like that to me or any woman again, comprende Mr Sean.' 'Comprende Maria, comprende.' 'Let's dance.'

***

'The waiters were walking around with champagne on their golden trays, and I took two flutes of champagne from

159

one of the waiters. 'Mmmmm, this taste excellent Maria, I have never tasted champagne like this before, come to think of it, I have never tasted champagne before. 'Mr Sean, this champagne cost $20,000 per bottle.

'And how many bottles are here, Maria?' 'About 30,000 bottles.

'Fecking hell Maria, that's £600,000 alone on champagne, never mind all the other drinks here, plus the food as well, how the other half live, eh.'

The night was ending, but I have not seen Phil for about 4 hours; I hope the Mexican bandits have not harmed him? The Mexican cartels are a bunch of murderers, they skin people alive, then hang them from bridges, to make a point, or they dissolve them in *acid*, they kill everybody connected to the person they have just killed, their fathers, mothers brothers, and sisters, they even kill the family pets; as I said before they make the 'Waffen ss" look like altar boys, they are the evilest people to walk God's earth, I do hope Phil's good, or big boy going to have to go into combat- mode.

'Where the hell have you been Phil, it's 8 am, I have been looking for you all night,' 'Sorry Mr Sean, but I have seen the *vampire and werewolf* with my own eyes, your right Mr Sean, and I took a video of them on my mobile phone, Blackie and one of the Mexicans were in the stables arguing with a Colombian Senate guy.' how did you know he was a Colombian senate guy? Because he came up to me and introduced himself as senator Restrepo, and said are you from Scotland? I said; indeed, I am, sir.' He replied, your English is excellent. I did not know what to make of that comment Mr Sean.

Phil dinnae worry about it mate, most people here probably think we are all Haggis farmer in Scotland and ride big Clydesdale horses, wearing face-paint and kilts shouting Freedom, either that, or he was taking the piss out you mate, sorry for interrupting you Phil, please continue. Blackie then changed into the *werewolf*, ripped his throat out, and without touching, he lifted the guy ten feet off the ground. Then the Mexican turned into the *vampire* plunged his claws into his chest, and pulled his heart out and opened his mouth ten times the average size and ate it, then picked up the body, and flew out the stable door with it; look have a look-see at the video yourself.

See then Phil let's have a look-see, god that horrific, look at the size of them, and muscle mass on them, they look like they have been on the steroids, they must have terrorized the Inca people with their body mass. The way they attacked that guy must have had the Inca shivering to the bone with fear, and Blackie changed back as fast as, so they must be able to change whenever they want to and, I bet all off Pablo's sicarios worldwide are like that, they must be hundreds of them, remember Phil acted like nothing had happened ok', our lives depend on it, fuck this is crazy did they see you.'

No, I was up in the hayloft, *"A chilling fear worked down my spine after watching the video.*

These werewolves and vampires if these have had sex with other humans, which no doubt they have their DNA, have mixed with human DNA.

Send the video to my mobile phone Phil, Was Lucianna there with you, 'No Mr Sean she was getting some drink from the party, we drank three bottles of that champagne, plus Lucianna had some Marijuana.' 'What are you smoking that shit for Phil.'

'A wee bit of grass will do you no harm Mr Sean.' 'Marijuana is the gateway to other drugs, Phil.

'What you mean by that, Mr Sean?'

'Well think about it Phil, most people smoke Marijuana dope, hash, Buda, call it what you like, then, they may go onto harder drugs like heroin, cocaine, crystal meth, opioid painkillers, etc., etc., etc., then the drugs get a hold of you, and it's hard as hell to get off them, you'll become a drug addict, and what do you think Pablo would say if he found out that you were smoking grass with Lucianna? Pablo and his Olmec cartel, the Mexican cartel, and all off the other cartels in the Americas are the tools of Satan, and they are the banality of evil, and not to mention, you had three bottles of champagne! 'What, three fecking bottles, that's £60,000 worth of champagne, yourself and Lucianna swallowed, please, please, please, tell me you never touched her. Phil!'

"Some people have big ears; some people have small ears, and some people have shit for brains."

Well, Mr Sean put it this way; what has Luisanna and jelly got in common.

I dinnae ken, Phil?

Both wriggle when you eat them.

Feck sake dinnae let Pablo hear you saying that you are joking Phil, aren't you?

'Mr Sean, these things just happened.' 'No fucking way did you make out with her?'

'Yes, I did.'

'For fuck sake, I told you, do not look or touch any female's here, but no, not you; you had to make out with Pablo Escobar, fucking daughter, thank God nobody seen you.'

'Do you think she tells her dad Phil?' 'No, but.' 'No but what Phil?' 'Mahmoud came into the stables; he was watching myself and Lucianna on the closed-circuit TV.' 'Do you think he'll say anything to Pablo?' 'Course he will, for fuck sake, we're up shit creek now, no thanks to you, you fucking stupid cunt, we were going to be going home back tae Dundee later today.'

'What do you think Pablo will say, Mr Sean?'

'Well, Phil, he will say welcome to the family Phil, thank god it was you and not that Mr Sean, he looks a bit off a numpty, and once again thank you very much for smashing the feck out of my daughter, here "£300 million, one million for every time you gyrated your hips" and don't bother about the airline tickets, you can take my private plane, over to Scotland and one more thing, here is the keys to my fucking super mansion I have just built, and before you go, you can help yourself to my private collection of antiquities Phil, what tae fuck do you think he's going to say?'

Sorry, Mr Sean, she remembers me of that girl from Dryburgh Alison Smowey, you remember her Mr Sean.

Course I do she was the tart of Dundee, she seen more cock-end that week-ends, she screwed everybody', she was with every gang member in Dundee, a person only had to look at her and her knicker were right off, she was going out with a farmer's son, and he filmed her having sex with a horse, bent over the stable doors she has to be dead now Phil.'

She's not mate, she's working as a chemist assistant, in one of the prominent chemists in the town.

Sorry Mr Sean, but with everything that has just happened, I had just lost control of my thoughts.'

Yes, Phil and your hormones took over?

It's not every day you see a *werewolf and vampire, kill someone, do you!*

I guess you're right, Phil, but ha-ho, and Phil, you will have to get your eyes tested mate.'

Because Lucianna looks feck all like Alison Smowey, is a fecking dog mate.

(*The lonesome boatman coming tae get you*) 'Just then, we can hear the footsteps running along the corridor, then the door bursts opened

all the fucking sicarios were in Phil's room now, they never said anything, they grabbed both of us and bundled the two of us downstairs, into a big room were Don Pablo and Santiago was standing. *The shit's going to hit the fan now, feck his forehead veins are about to pop.*

'Don Pablo can I just say ...' 'Mr Sean, don't speak until your spoken too, and you Phil don't say a fucking word or my Sicario's will drop the both of you where you stand, I invited both of you into my home and Phil, you pay me back with forcing yourself on my Lucianna, this is how you return my hospitality. You see, Pablo was mad, the white of his eyes was all bloodshot.

Maria had just come in. 'Please Don Pablo, have mercy on them.' The fear on her face says it all, something bad was going to happen, then, the Mexican murdering bastard had to get his word in.

'Please Pablo, let me take care of these two pieces of shit, my sicarios are Experts in Mutilation and Torture, it would be a great pleasure to take care of them for you. *fuck that's heavy* My sicario's will cut off their ears and nose's and their testicles and make a chain so that you can put it around your big white monkey's neck Pablo.

'Santiago, Kong is not a monkey, he's across river gorilla, and for your information, Kong mate, Jane is pregnant, if everything goes good, it will be the first time a cross-river gorilla has ever been born in captivity. Kong, he is the rarest in the world and never call Kong a monkey again!'

Santiago quickly corrected himself. 'One thousand's apologizes boss.

'This is my present to you, Santiago, take Phil and do what you want to him, you may say your good-byes to Mr Sean and as for you Mr Sean, you are going home.

'Thank you very much, Don Pablo, but I came here with Phil, and I am not leaving without him, if you are going to kill Phil, then you have to kill me as well Pablo.

'You are either a fearless man, Mr Sean, or a foolish one.

Maria quickly chips in to save our head. 'Please, Don Pablo, it's just human nature, you cannot keep your daughters virgin's forever, they have to Experience love, do you remember your first-time Pablo.' 'Yes, I do, Maria. *I think he's calming down now.*

'The dead only know one thing Mr Sean, it's better to be alive, I have made my decision, both of you will be taken from here to the airport, to catch a flight back home to Dundee but first I want both of you to deliver something, two suitcases of high-quality Columbian snow (cocaine) for me, if you refuse, my sicarios will fill you and your family body full of holes, so much that there will be whistling when they're getting pushed through the morgue. Mr Sean, Phil, remember I have your home addresses back in Dundee. Plato un plomo, *which means it's either silver or lead, take the silver, or we will kill you,* here is one silver dollar, the Dominions are falling, they will soon reach the end! Aurevoir Mr Sean, Phil, you don't have to be a Danny dyers all your life's.

Pablo looks at us like lost souls. 'The pair of you are a blot on one's Escutcheon. I would shake your hand, Mr Sean, but your hands are dirty, Mr Sean.

'The dirt's not on my hands Pablo, it's in your fucking soul!'

And that was it, with one nod of his head we had been throwing into the back of a jeep, but I still had time to kiss Maria and to tell her I would never forget her.

***

We were being driving through the main town and then through the outskirts, then into the "Barrios" (shanty town) the journey seems to last forever, then we stopped outside this old, dilapidated house.

As we had been ushered inside, there were four more of Pablo's henchmen, and an older woman tells us to take off our tops while one of the henchmen looks at us. 'One of the sicarios said you would not be wearing these again.

As he handed myself and Phil what looked like bulletproof vests; Put them on now, but they were not bulletproof vests, they were full of cocaine, as we put them on, the older woman started to sew the front of the vest, so there no way myself or Phil can take them off, then we were handed two xxx L Aloha shirts. 'Put these on; they will help hide the vests.' Afterward, it was back in the jeep and off to the airport. One of Don Pablo's harsh looking man gave us further instruction, 'go to the main desk there, and you will be handed tickets for your return journey back home, you will be watching you every step of the way.

How are you bearing up to it, Phil?

I am shitting myself, Mr Sean.

Phil, from now on, act and talk like this is an everyday occurrence; this is the only way we are going to get through this mess, Phil, ok.'

'Sure, here Mr Sean, these vests fit tighter than *OJ CLOVE!*' (THE *DUICE*)

'Yes, Phil, but *OJ* had the best legal team money can buy, we would need Merlin the magician to get out of this fine mess you have gotten us into.' .

Do you think he did it, I mean *OJ* did the two murderers? Remember, they played the 911 police calls, and you heard him beating on his wife.

Yes I know Phil but not every man that hits his woman, does not go on to kill her, and another thing Is he was found not guilty, and not unless his hands double in size since the murders, remember the saying *if the gloves don't fit you have to acquit*, that will do me mate, anyway he was a hero to most African-Americans, Just a normal boy that became an American football legend, I see the program about it on tv, most people saying it was justice for *the L A* riots in 1992, three years before the *OJ* trial, let's concentrate in getting through customs, and getting back home to Dundee Phil ok.'

Yes, sure, Mr Sean, and bring this Colombian trip to a close.

Phil their never no closure, closure, was invented by people that never had bad times, mate, everything comes back and haunt you like a *jimmy Savile rape*, mate.

"Pressure makes diamonds."

Everybody in the airport was smiling at the two of us, and now, this is when you start to get paranoid, thinking everybody knows we are carrying drugs, we were, we are drug mules, we've never touched cocaine before. Now, we're moving about 50 kgs each of the shit.

'I don't think I can do this, Mr Sean.'

'Phil, you have to stay focused, think P.M. A.

'Yeah, what's P.M. A?' Phil asks me.

'Positive mental attitude, look, Phil, let's go to the bathroom and splash our faces with some cold water and get focused. We're going to walk through the eye of the needle, and I'll go first Phil, if anything happens, you don't know me, and I don't know you, go for it Phil, and remember we are not Like Evil Knievel, we're not getting paid for the attempt; this is the real Phil.

'Yeah, Mr Sean.' 'Well, let's go and get this over and done with.

'Sure thing, big boy. 'Stop calling me big boy!

The hardest part was checking in the bags, and then going through the security, 20 minutes till our plane takes off, that was the longest 20 minutes of my life.

'Made it, seat number 50 A and seat number 51 B, I've got the window seat, Mr Sean.'

'Pull down the blinds, and I never want to see Columbia again, in 24 hours we will be back home In Dundee Phil, look at the big smile on your face Phil.'

It's a mirror image of the smile on your face big boy, and we're going home, we're going home.

Then it happened, the army and FIVE-0 were over the plane like a "blizzard," we were marched off the plane and lead through the airport, everybody was looking at myself and Phil.

Now, even the police were smiling, giving each other high fives, *the game was over, a new chapter in our lives was about to start.*

***

The Lawyer 'Mr Sean, Phil, let me introduce myself, my name is macro Gomez, I am the lawyer that is appointed to represent both of you on two counts of drug trafficking 213 kgs of pure Columbia snow (cocaina).'

'Why is cocaine called Columbia snow Mr Sean?'

'Because it never snows here in Columbia and everyone like snow.'

'Mr Gomez, we were set up for this.'

'Please, Mr Sean, Phil, call me Marco.' 'Ok Marco, as I was saying we were set up to smuggle this cocaine back into Scotland by Pablo Escobar.'

'Are you talking about the one and only Pablo Escobar, the richest man in the world?'

(Cocaine infiltrates all forms of society like cancer) 'Yes, we are, so we started from the beginning and told Marco everything from the first meeting with Pablo till why we are here, talking to him.

'I see, the both of you, are north of the border and south of the Equator, you have a poor hand, and not very many cards to play with, corpus delicti, Mr Sean, it has already been proven, yourself and Phil caught with 213 kg, of pure cocaina, Columbian snow. Do not tell anybody what you have told me, Pablo has ears everywhere, here in Columbia, I have never like Pablo, he has the blood of my best friend on his hands, well, his sicario's does, I will try and help you in every way.

'Yes, But Marco, we have not been interviewed by the police yet.

'Mr Sean, this is a game to them; they are not bothered about where you got the drugs from, If both of you plead guilty, you will be sentenced to 5 years in jail, if you plead not guilty and you are found guilty, you will receive 13 years in prison.'

13 years, that ass-hole Pablo's favourite number again

'Well, it's a no-brainier Marco, we will plead guilty to drug smuggling, can you tell myself and Phil what's going to happen now?'

'Of course, Mr Sean, tomorrow the both of you will be showing in front of the world's media, and then you will be taking down to the holding cells the following day. Afterward, both of you will appear in the constitutional court of Colombia where I will tender you plea of guilty to two counts of drug-Smuggling. Then, the Prosecutor will outline the case to the judge, and the judge will deliver his sentence by letter to me the next day, where I will come to you and Inform the both of you, the judge's decision, it will be fast-tracked, It will all be over in 48 hours.

'Ok then, Marco, so how do we pay for your services?'

'do not worry, Mr Sean, Phil, I have already been paid.' 'By whom Marco?' 'By Maria.

Next day, we were showing off to the press like two common drug smugglers, the world press was there with the television cameras as well beaming our faces all over every paper and news stations in the world.

We are in jail now down on our knuckles. 'This is the lowest point in our lives, but we will come through it, remember P.M.A?' 'What tae feck P.M.A Mr Sean?'

'Phil, "positive mental attitude," I have told you this before, do you not listen?'

'Oh, sorry, I forgot.'

'don't fecking listen, you don't if you do, we won't be in this fecking mess.'

'We have good survival instincts, and we are going to need them all, the jails here are not going to be like Perth, Saughton or Barlinnie (jails in Scotland), the next 24 hours, it will all be over, there are two rules in jail, Phil, rule number one, trust no one, and what's rule number two Mr Sean, see rule number one Phil.'

Do you not trust me then Mr Sean?

Phil, at this moment in time, I don't even trust myself mate, but saying that I do trust you to fuck up everything that you do, mate!

We are in the holding cell with about ten other people, and all harden criminals, this guy comes up to myself and Phil. 'hello, I am Edison, we all seen the pair off you on tv last night, you two are drug smugglers.

'Your powers of observation astonished me, Edison, yes we are, and we will know our punishment in the next 24 hours.'

'The pair of you better hope you are not going to Riohacha prison; this is one of the worst jail here in Colombia. The gang that runs the jail, the leader, is how you would say like a male company.

'So, he's Homosexual, Edison.'

'Yes, you will have to kneel in front of him and suck him off, or his men will cut your throat.

'Fuck that Edison, if anybody puts his penis in my mouth, I will fecking bite it off.

Phil responds to me, with his cheeky smirk on his face. 'Yeah sure, Mr Sean, after 20 minutes.'

'Feck off Phil, you know this is like a fucking nightmare, it's like the police and army at the airport knew we were coming, even as soon as we got off the plane, you never told anybody that we were coming to Colombia did you?'

'Phil!' 'no, not really Mr Sean.' 'What do you mean not really, Phil?' 'Well, I let it slip when I was talking to Snelly.

'No fucking way you told Snelly Mo' Mo, fecking hell, three ways of communication in the world,

1. *TELEPHONE,*
2. *TELEVISION,*
3. *TELL SNELLY MO'MO.*

He's got a big mouth, and I can't believe you told him for feck's sake.

'I am sorry, Mr Sean.'

'It's ok, saying that now Phil, you will be ok in jail.' 'Howz that Mr Sean? You got my back.

'No, I will be holding you down while the guys smash feck out of your ass.

'My anal virginity will not last an hour in jail look at me, man.

'Remember what you said to me Phil, a little bit of brownnnn never let you downnnnnnnnnnnnn.

They will not be looking at your ball- sack In the shower mate, it will be your arse, Phil, so watch yourself in jail, I 've got your back, and you have got mines, comprende Phil?

Si Baroni, I can do that, Mr Sean, I got dressed all by myself this morning!

Phil why are you taking the piss mate, 'I wish I took Pablo's offer now.' 'What offer was that Mr Sean?'

'Pablo offer me £ 13 million to shoot you because he wanted to add your head to his collection of shrunken heads.

'What tae fuck, Mr Sean, why did you not tell me!'

'And if I did tell you, would you go into combat-mode and wipe him out and all of his fecking sicarios, you would have "shit a brick mate," that's why I never told you.

'Hahaha, I am only joking with the two of you, just a little Columbian humour. *Edison suddenly chips in.*

'You cunt, Edison, you had me thinking there, the FARC (*the FARC is a guerrilla movement involved in the continuing Colombian armed conflict from 1964-2017, one of the riches freedom fighting group in the world*).

The FARC controls all the high-security jail here in Columbia, as part of the peace proses, the FARC lay down their arms and was given, 15 seats in the Columbian Senate. As part of the proses, they have to spend some time in jail where they are being educated because most of the fighters have never been to school, fighting the Columbian army is all most of them did, now, they spend at least three days in jail per week, they are not being punished, but been educated, they are learning to read, write, and they are learning trades like saying, plumbing, carpentry, electricians, there are even some rebel fighters taking lawyers courses, some of these FARC rebel fighters have a very high level of IQ, most people agree to "farc" being part of the government but some people disagree.

'You cannot put a price on peace, Mr Sean.

(There are always innocent people that get killed in war)

***

The next day, we were taken from the holding cells and brought up to the supreme court.

In the court, there was the judge, procurator, stenographer, and Mr Gomez, me and Phil, and about 11 policeman-woman. Mr Gomez enter our pleads, the procurator outline the case to the judge, the judge says he will announce his decision in two hours by letter to Mr Gomez, that was the most prolonged two hours we ever had to wait, a policeman came into the cell, *(all smiles fecking pound land Colombo)* 'Mr Sean, Phil, Mr Gomez is in the interview room down the corridor; please follow me.

'As we walked through the door, Mr Gomez was sitting behind the table with five policemen behind him, and I am very sorry, Mr Sean, Phil, you have been sentenced to 55 years.

'No fucking way man, fifty-five (55) years, you said if we pleaded guilty, we were looking at five years.

'Please let me finish Mr Sean; the procurator wanted to send a message to would-be "drug smugglers," that it cannot be or will not be tolerated.

'We know that fecking judge and procurator, they were the same guy's that I saw when I walked into a room in Pablo's house, and they were snorting cocaine off the naked body of a girl, the pair of them are fecking pot-licker. And the other two guys were giving two young girls a *Colombian snowstorm*.

We were not transferred to a high-security prison, but a low-security one, the name of the jail translated into English, is El-shite-hole.

The police car pulled up to this old pair of rusty gates the walls were about 15 feet high, stretching around the perimeter of the jail.

We will walk out of this place, Phil. I can guarantee you that, mate. Let's hope so big boy, or in 55 years, we will be getting a push out in a wheelchair.

'Here is your new home, one of the policemen said, smirking, enjoy your stay, as we walk through the gates, we knew this was dilapidated old jail, overcrowded, with hundreds of people, murderers, thief's, rapists every low life in Columbia was here, the prison guards took everything we owned, the chief guard pulled the ring from Phil's finger. 'If you give this to me, you will have an easy time here, but if I must take it from you, you will not have a good time here.

'I hope you enjoy your new ring.' Phil said, smiling to his new friend.

'My name is Rahul, I am the head guard in this prison, you will not be bothered by anybody here, but do not break the rules, or we will break you. Please put on these two black armbands, and it will tell the prisoners and guard alike that the pair of you are under my protection now, you can keep your money, you will need it.

'Now, that guard knew that ring was worth money, let hope he stays around for a while, eh, Phil?'

As we walked into our new home, 'here, Mr Sean, I've just noticed, where is your ring?'

'Phil, I suitcase it.

You suitcase it what do you mean by that Mr Sean?

Phil, I put the ring up my ass when we were on the plane, we are going to need all the money we can, because I am not staying here in this fucking shit hole for the next fifty-five (55) fecking years because you could not keep your c*ck in your fecking boxer short.

(you can always bet on the Crumlin kangaroos)

Money buys you everything in jail, food, clothes, toiletry, even a single cell will cost you $15 per week. We had about

£400, between both of us, the first four weeks we had to share a cell with 40 other people, with one toilet, with an old holed curtain for privacy, it's funny, last week, we were sitting on a gold toilet in the lap of luxury, now we are sharing this toilet that never flushed, we had one pale of water to wash away the faeces and urine, that the guards handed in twice a day, the smell was horrendous,(*far worse than Phil's smelly feet*), and as for the beds, well there was no beds, all the prisoners had a piece of cardboard laid on the ground, and their cloth was used, for the blankets.

The only good/safe place in jail is in the hospital especially if you have a mental illness, and it's like a 5-star hotel compared to the rest of the prison, Pablo Escobar takes great pride in looking after people with mental illness.

The second day in jail, a prisoner came into the cell, and the other prisoners just pounced on him, beating him up and dragged him out to the prison yard, where they're a child paddling pool, full of dirty water, the other prisoner held his head under the water until he was dead.

A lot of Pablo's political enemies, were in this jail as well, *"prisoners of conscience"* all of Pablo's political enemies, had to wear a red armband, there where, New prisoners coming in every day, you would see a prisoner with the red armband on and then the next week, he was nowhere to be seen, most night while you were in the cell there was always some commotion, in the yard late at night, you could hear the people screaming, in pain then there was an eerie silence, I did ask the other prisoners about the screaming outside, but they said that they never heard anything. Still, you could tell the prisoner knew that something was going on in the yard, but they were too scared to talk about it.

Welcome to your new home gentlemen, as myself and Phil turned around, we were greeted by a black guy holding out his hand, my name is john j' everybody calls me Rambo.

My name is Mr Sean, and this is Phil.' Yes, I know who the both of you are.

So, Rambo, what is a 6'7 American guy like you doing here in Colombia?

18 months ago, I was part of a crack Navy Seal unit, for a top-secret covert mission to find and Kill Pablo Escobar; he was staying at his luxury villa in Cartagena in Colombian, we flew under the Radar by helicopter, to our drop location, but as soon as we landed, we were attacked by a wolf-like Creatures, 14 men the finest soldiers the USA has ever seen, wiped out in 45 seconds, 13 men Lay dead their bodies mutilated, unrecognizable, only there dog-tags left by their bodies, which I have now in my cell; hopefully, I will be able to give them to the soldiers' families.

Sorry to hear about your friends.

They all knew the dangers of joining up, that one day they may be killed, but they never expected To be killed in such a horrific way, I seen it all with my own eyes, blood, flesh, heads cracked Opened like eggs with their brains spilled out all over the ground, not one of the creatures came Near me, it was like they had to keep a witness, someone to tell the story, just like I am telling you.

That's horrific john j' so how long are you in here for?

I have been told that I will be going home to the USA very soon, so I can say to the president of The United States, what has happened to his elite Navy Seal soldiers, we were the most magnificent fighting unit the world has ever seen, we had been on countless mission around the world, our greatest mission of them all, operation *Neptune spear,* to take down Osama bin Laden the leader of Al-Qaeda, may 2nd 2011,14 men landed by chopper, in Bilal town, Pakistan, seven people killed, we were on the ground for 15 minutes, and not one Navy seal casualty, yet we land here in Columbia. We were all wiped out in seconds; I will have to go now. I must write a letter, and I will see you all soon.

Well, you will be because we are not going anywhere.

John j' Rambo, turned and smiled, that was the first and last time we saw him, he was never seen again, maybe he's back home?

Here, Mr Sean, I was thinking you were going to tell him about the *werewolves and vampires.*

No fecking way, Phil, I am not telling anyone, and either is you well not until we are out of this place, ok.

You don't have to worry about that, Mr Sean.

The next morning, Mr Sean, I had a good dream last night, the first dream I had in here, you want to hear about it, mate?

Sure, enlighten my day can't wait to hear this one.

I had a dream last night that I was eating *Halle Berri pussy,* I was at this Hollywood Oscars party, after the Oscars obviously, and we got talking and she invited me back to her mansion in *Beverly Hills.'*

Are you sure it was not a nightmare?

A nightmare? Making out with 24-year-old *Halle Berri,* she is Beautiful, mate.

Yes I know she's a honey, not a nightmare for you, but it would be for *Halle Berri,* I can see her now telling all her superstars and celebrity friends, while having lunch, at the best restaurant in Beverly Hills, *I had a horrible nightmare, last night girls, do you remember they two white tattie picking Niggas from Scotland, that have been all over the news last month international drug smuggling in Colombia, smuggling that "Bolivian marching powder," well I had a nightmare the one of the guy's Phil, you know, He looks like Keanu I don't like him as an actor. Still, I do like him as a person, I turned down the leading lady in a film with him, I did not want to do it, girls, well he was eating my pussy, that's enough to put you off sex for life, what a nightmare, but on the other hand if it was his friend Mr Sean, he sure is a sweetie-pie, girls and I know myself and Mr Sean can do some serious business between the sheet in my four-poster bed, but not before we had shared the hot-tub drinking a bottle of 1820 Juglar Cuvee, yes girls that would be a moment I will cherish for the rest of my life.'*

Yeah sure Mr Sean your like my granny's cat, mate full "o" wind and pish, Halle does nae ken what a tattie picker is mate, she's probably never seen a tattie before, the closest she's been to a potato is when she been eating *French fries with a medium-rare venison steak,* at one of the top a la carte restaurants in Los Angeles, and another think "Mr big-headed Sean," I forgot when you die mate, you are Donating your body to science, just so the scientist can work out what makes 'Mr Sean, 'Mr Sean, the eighth wonder of the world, a handsome, gifted Greek god, looks off Adonis *god of beauty "o lord it's hard to be humble when your perfect in every way,"* and so nobody feels hard-done-by, every university in Scotland getting two inches of you penis, and the other 10 inches are getting raffled off for a good cause.

No, Phil, the other 10 inches is getting, given to your sister so she can keep it under her pillow at Night time mate, *the tail doesn't wag the dog, the dog wags the tail, Phil,* anyway, why are you dreaming About *Halle Berri,* mate, you are a racist person Phil?

I am not a racist person Mr Sean, remember I've got a black and white tv remember, and why are you acting like the world should be proud to have you here on Earth? You're not the hokey pokey kid; you're not what it's all about, mate.

There's only one kind of man/woman in this world, you either believe in yourself, or you don't it's as simple as that Phil, I never said I was Phil, but unlike you, I stop and think, If you stopped and think, we would be back in Dundee now sitting with at least a few £million in the bank after selling the two rings, but no not you, you had to charge in with your trouser down, and look where we are now, one of the worst jails in the Americas, amnesty international has Condemned this jail as one off the worst prisons, in the world so don't be having a go at me, mate ok!

Sorry, Mr Sean; I guess I am jealous of you because of your confidence and good self-esteem. I wish that I had what you have, mate, I do.

Well, Phil, you dinnae have it mate, so suck it up yae pussy, only joking mate, too be confident you have to believe in yourself and to build confidence, all you have to do is to go out of your comfort zone just a little each day mate, building confidence does not happen, overnight mate, you have to work at it, and as for self-esteem, keep on telling yourself that you are the greatest person ever to walking this earth now, this is the first time you have told me this Phil, that's good you see you are starting to build confidence now you see if as straightforward as that mate.

So is that how you get your confidence and self-esteem, Mr Sean, I wish I had told you this before, mate.

Phil, I am only taking the piss out of you mate, you will always be a fecking loser mate.

You are a fecking bastard, Mr Sean, here me thinking I'm going to mould myself into a new person, and you are making a fool out of me, "cunt."

'Phil, just follow what I have just said, and before long you will be where you want tae be mate, now come here and give me a man hug, but remember one thing, Phil.'

And that is Mr Sean?

No tongues now come here yae big "duine eireachdail" bastard and Gee 'us a man hug and remember Phil dinnae lose yer Heid.

"The thing of been a loser is you don't have anything to lose in the first place."

It would be four weeks until we have moved to our private cell thanks to our new friend, Rahul.'

'The cell was far better than the one we had to stay in for the last four weeks, it had a small cooker, plates, cutlery, cups, and an old kettle, the mattresses were all stain with urine, faeces, and vomit, and no doubt, the other stains were semen, you had to pay the guards for blankets, the cell was a shit hole, but it was far better than the first one we were in, and there was one key to the cell door, And it had to be locked at all times because even though we were in a better part of the jail, other prisoners would take, steal anything, it was just a way of life in here, and when the door was locked, you had to keep anything out of arms reach, or someone would put their hands through the bars and steal it, six bars on the window where the warm breeze came through, but it was better than nothing.

Late at night, Mr Sean, Mr Sean, wake up *Phil keep on pushing me,* blooded hell Phil I was having a good sleep, what is it?

There here.

Who's here, Phil?

The *Vampires,* like human creatures, I've seen them with my own eyes again.

How, where, when Phil?

Outside in the prison yard, I was lying in my bed, it must have been about 4 am, And I heard a bit of commotion, so I looked out the window cell bars, but the commotion was, To the right, so I got my small shaving mirror, and put it at an angled it to see what was happening, And Rahul the head guard was standing, with another prison guard, they were standing talking to one of Pablo's political prisoner, and all of a sudden Rahul changed into, one of the fecking *vampire's* And ripped his throat out, and the other guard, who had also changed' grabbed him, before he Hit the ground, flew out of the prison yard with him, it all happened so fast, Mr Sean.

For fuck sake, how many of the *vampires* are they, here in Colombia?

This must be how Pablo, killing his political prisoner and enemies. *Pablo's political prisoners were given a hard time, they're second to the third day, here they are tortured, by means of getting water throwing over them, and the guard would use cattle-prods on them you knew by the screaming, that it was excruciating, after that they would be given a severe beating, then put back into the prison population, most of these prisoners would be given 15 to life.* Still, in a matter of days, they would be never be seen again. all those *vampires and werewolves," ancient Aliens" are under Pablo's command,* who knows how Many he has working for him, Phil, did they see you at any point, Phil?

No, no way man not, unless they can see around corners.

Phil, they could have seen you in the reflection of the mirror, mate.'

Sorry I am a bit uptight now Mr Sean, do you think Pablo has the same fate in store for you and me?

No Phil if he did, we would have been dead a long time ago, mate.

What are we going to do now, Mr Sean?

Nothing Phil, we can't do feck all mate, we will have to wait until we try and get out of here ourselves, have you noticed something different about this prison, Phil?

No, what is it, Mr Sean?

Well with, Colombian being such a religious country Phil, there no church here in prison, and I have Never seen a priest here either, so they fear something to do with the church.

But what Mr Sean, at Pablo's place, there was a church, a Tabernacle, altar and crucifix, and there was even a priest father, Makie Murphy.

There must be something Phil; there always is, did you not say that Pablo was wearing contact lenses?

Yes, Mr Sean and the rest of his sicario's as well, and Rahul and the guards wear them too, as I said before my sister wears them, I know if someone got contact lenses a mile off, mate.

So, they must be special lenses they are wearing to shield their eyes from?

It must be something to do about the sun, Mr Sean.

That would make a lot of sense Phil would it, the sunlight must be too strong for them, and another thing, they must only be able to change in the dark, the sunlight must affect their ability to change in Day time, anyway, that's not our problemo, we have to concentrate on getting out of here, and back home, Phil.

Yeah I know mate, six weeks ago we were back home in Dundee, not a care in the world, now look where we are now 55 years in this shit hole of a jail, set up as two drug mules, not to mention these *werewolves and vampires,* and god knows what else is in store for myself and you Mr Sean, I feel now that I am ready for anything that comes my way.

Right Phil, take everything head-on fuck it.

(Every night the killing when on)

Morning Phil, you grind your teeth when you are sleeping it's most annoying, listening to you grin your teeth all night and another thing Phil, were you cracking one off last night mate?

Noooo, not me, Mr Sean, why?

You better known be mate, while I'm in bed next to you, that not normal doing that while another

Guy's in the same room.'

What's your fecking problem, Mr Sean, type of guy you think I am, cracking one-off in the same room as you mate anyway If I did, I wouldnae be thinking of you any mate.'

Yeah, bet you say that to all the boy's Phil.'

Spin-on it, Mr Sean.

You can but anything you want in this place, the main man here for buying anything is a guy called "Adentric," he was the normal run of the mill jail guy, you would not trust him as far as you could throw him but if you needed to buy something, he's the man to See.

'Hello, Adentric; I was told you are the man to see if I need to buy any goods here in jail.'

'Yes, you are Mr Sean, and your friend is Phil, the two of you are drug smugglers.'

'We are innocent.' 'Yes, Mr Sean, and so is everybody in here.'

'"whatever" Adentric, can you get two mattresses covers?' 'Yes, Mr Sean, why do you need them? is it because you are incontinent?'

'No, Adentric.' *Cheeky bastard.* 'It's because the mattresses are all covered in dodgy stains.'

'Mr Sean, this is not a hotel, it's a prison.' 'Can you get them, yes or no?' 'Yes, I can, it will take a few days, is there any special Colours you wish for?' *Is he taking the piss?* 'No, just anyone's will do, for now, Adentric.

It would be a few more days till we got our food to cook in the cell, the guards were the people to buy the food from, and it all came at an extortionate price, but it is far better than the food in the jail, the food in jail was awful, only the people that never had any money would eat it, you had to stand in line until it was your turn to get your food from an old plate with a dollop of what I can only describe as brown porridge, some prisoners would add insects to it for more of a better taste, there was a lot of people getting stabbed, due to the fact, people were stealing food, and like all prisons all over the world, drugs were sold, the drug was mainly sold by the prison guards, heroin, cocaine, marijuana.

'Adentric.' 'Yes Mr Sean, what can I do you for?' (*He always says this to people who are going to buy from him*) 'I would like to buy a mobile phone.' 'A mobile phone, Mr Sean?' 'sorry, Adentric, cell phone. 'Yes, of course, Mr Sean.' 'And wait, there is more, I would also like an international phone card. 'I can have them here in 2 days cool and price for you, my friend is $100.

'Fuck, that's highly expensive, at least Dick Turpin wore a mask when he robbed people.'

'Who is this Dick Turpin, Mr Sean?'

(*Dick Turpin was an English highwayman whose exploits were exaggerated following his execution in the city of York for horse theft, he was hanged by the neck until dead in the year 1739.*)

'It's just a saying we say back home in Britain, Adentric.' 'The price is still the same Mr Sean, $100, $80 for cell phone and $20 for a phone card.' 'That's with $20 credit as well, Adentric?'

'Yes, Mr Sean.' 'Two days, remember, don't tell anyone, Adentric.' 'Why? Most people here have them; I will do Mr Sean.

'Here, Phil, I have ordered a mobile phone with a phone card from Adentric.

'How much did you get them for Mr Sean?'

'$100.' 'Feck, that will be most of our money gone.' '$100 is nothing unless you'll like to stay here for the next fecking 55 years, I will tell you later Phil, I have to plan this out.

'I was talking to Adentric, one of the prisoners.' 'That's the same guy that we are buying the phone from Phil.' 'Mr Sean, small world then, and he'd have a sister, he says I can write to her and hopefully, get to know her, maybe she can come here to visit the both of us in jail.'

'Sure, Phil, but don't say anything about trying to escape, because the guards read all the letters, remember the rules in here, trust nobody, fuck it, I don't even trust myself sometimes Phil.

'Nice one Mr Sean, nice one big boy.

'Phil, knock it on your head, stop calling me big boy.

'Hahaha, will do Mr Sean, will do.' 'What is Adentric sister called?' 'She called Nikki, Mr Sean.

'Nikki, sticky Nikki, bet she's a big fatty and will have about four children, you will be the long-lost uncle Phil.' 'Ha ha ha, very funny Mr Sean.' 'I don't see a stampede of a girl coming to see you here. 'Maria will come.' 'I know she will, Phil.

'Mr Sean, here is your cell phone you ordered.' 'Thank you, Adentric.

The mobile phone was just a basic one, back home, it would cost about £5 from anywhere in the UK but not here, $80 is a small price for freedom though.

Now, this is going to be the hardest phone call that I have ever had to make, but it needs to be done.

Here goes, +44 1382 the home number 8__0___9___.

Ring, ring, ring........ 'Hello, dad, it's Sean.' 'What have you been up to, drug smuggling in Columbia, cocaine, the devil powder, you told everybody that yourself and Phil were going on holiday to Spain.

'Dad look, we were set up to smuggle drug by Pablo Escobar. 'It does not matter now Sean, it's been all over the papers, and on TV, 55 years in jail, the press and TV crews have been camped outside the house ever since the news broke.

'Are you trying to put your mother and me in an early grave, Sean?'

'No Dad, it's a long story, but myself and Phil are going to escape, let me finish dad, I need you to tell Tone and Brian (my brothers) to come out here to visit me because I have a ring that was giving to me by that "cunt" Pablo "fucking" Escobar and it worth maybe £2 million ($3,000,000,000), I need you to sell it, for whatever you get for it because we need money here to survive, and to put the escape plan into action 'Sean, we have some money saved up, your brothers will be out there in a couple of weeks, the British embassy has been in touch with Patty and Gill (Phil's mum and dad), they were the ones who notified the family about the arrests for drug smuggling, seemingly the Columbian government, informed the British government here, but they never got in contact with anybody here.' 'Yeah, dad, that's because I travelled here on my Irish passport (*I've got dual nationality, my dad's from the island of Ireland*), dad, I am going to have to go, tell everybody not to worry, and I hope to see everybody soon.

'Take care, son, hope to see you and Phil soon. 'ok, dad, bye for now (*my dad or mum never calls me Mr Sean, they just call me Sean*).'

Five (5) days later. 'Phil, I've got good news, my brothers will be here tomorrow at about 2 pm. I've just got a text from the tone, and they are here in Colombia.

The next day.

'Mr Sean good news, you have visitors, here, they are your brothers from Scotland.' 'Thank you, Rahul.' 'Mr Sean, you will have a private room here, where you can meet your brothers.

'once again, thank you, Rahul.

Rahul, is about 5-7 tall very dark complexion, jet black hair, I think he dyes his hair, he is very portly, about 14 stone in weight, always sweating, especial under his arms pits but one thing was he's looking after myself and Phil, we are given special privileges all the time.

'One more thing, Rahul, do you know Adentric sister, Nikki?' 'Yes, I do Nikki is a lovely looking girl, and she is a wonderful cake maker, she's all way baking cakes and handing them to the guards for their break time, why do you ask Mr Sean?'

'Because she will be writing and visiting Phil and myself.' 'one more thing, Mr Sean.

'You are allowed 30 minutes per visit, Mr Sean, and a guard will be outside the door at all times.

I stepped into the private room, where I saw my brothers already waiting for me. 'There's the man, long time no see bro, I was never so glad to see anybody before as my bro's walk in the room, that's a fine mess you and Phil has gotten into, dad told the two of us what happened, sean 'We were set up to smuggle drugs by the richest man in the world, Pablo Escobar.

'What to hell are you doing getting involved with him?'

'Long story, bro, but I will tell you all about it later, ok.' 'Dad said you had a ring that you wanted him to sell for you?' 'Yes, that's correct, look, this one will probably be the most expensive ring you'll ever see.' 'This is a lovely ring.' 'Yes, and these diamonds are the rarest in the world, yellow and red diamonds from the deepest mines in Botswana Africa, there's one thing though.

'And that is Sean? 'Don't put it in your mouth.' 'Why would I put it in my mouth anyway, sean?'

'I am just saying, don't because I had to hide it up to my "ass."

'Feck off, why did you have to hide it there?' 'Well, think about it, the police or the army, or the guards, would have confiscated it, won't they?' 'good thinking, sean.'

'Now, once dad's sell this ring to his antique dealers acquaintances, there will be money to help myself and Phil to get through living in this shit-hole of a jail, it's an uphill struggle going downhill in here anyway and hopefully, we plan to escape, they're all animals in here, just some have bigger teeth than others.

'How are you going to do that, Sean?'

'Well, tone, bri, the world cup finals are being played here in the Americas with games played in Columbia, Ecuador, Panama, Peru, and Venezuela, the finals kick off here in Columbia, six weeks, June 23rd and the semi-finals are being played in Columbia and Peru by July 10th with the world cup final been played 17th of July in Venezuela, that's where we make our escape from Venezuela.

'Yes, Sean but how to do you break out of this jail and get to Venezuela?' 'I have been thinking about this from "day dot," I don't want to go into details, let's just wait to see how much money we get for this ring, I will keep in contact with you all by phone, tell dad to buy three mobile phones and the next time I phone home, I will get the numbers.

'Time up, Mr Sean, your brothers, will have to leave.' 'That was quick, I am sorry Mr Sean, but you only get half an hour as Rahul told you.

I gave my brothers two-man hugs. 'Look after yourself Sean and tell Phil to keep his chin up, are you and Phil eating well in this place?

Well, the first time we had to eat in this place, talk about Delly belly, when you go to the toilet the world fall out your ass, "the food in here burns the hole aff ya" it is not good at all, so we have been buying in our food, with the little money we have.

'Will do tone.' 'Here, where's Phil, why is he not here?' 'He cannot come because it's a private visit.

'Here's £2,000 dad and mum gave you.' 'Great, this is going to help me out. I am going to buy a saxophone.' 'a saxophone! what the hell are you wanting to play the sax for, when you should be planning to escape.

'Tone, right, this is where the plan kicks off, once the pair of you get home, I need you to go to a music shop and buy a book about playing the saxophone.'

'But Sean, you have lots of books back home about playing the sax.' 'Yes, I know Bri, but I need you to get a book about playing the saxophone, but the book has to have a hardcover.

'Why's that Sean?' 'Wait, and I will tell you, Tone, I need you to buy 400 acid tablets (acid tablets LSD tablets, give the taker a hallucinogenic trip, a psychedelic experience (or trip), it's altered state of consciousness), remember the book about the sax, I need you to peel off the paper that covers the back of the book and get the acid-tablets and place them in single file on the hardback cover of the book, then glue the paper that you have just peeled off, back onto the hardcover. Make sure it's sealed good, then I want you to send me the book, with the acid tablets sealed in place, but don't send just one book, send about four books, so it looks just like a regular parcel of books, that anybody will get sent to them in jail. Oh and one more thing, send a book about Egyptian hieroglyphs.

Why a book on hieroglyphs Mr Sean?

Well I need something to absorb my mind with, and to knock the guards off the scent of the escape; 'Yes but wait a minute Sean, what about the customs here in Columbia, will they not check the parcel?' 'No Bri, nobody sends drugs into Columbia, most people smuggle drugs out of Columbia.

'Mr Sean times up.

My older brother Tone always remembers me of that survival Ventura, Bear Chills, you know the guy. He's always on television with some well-knowing TV celebrities that's never worked a day in their lives, taking them on some survival weekend that goes for Bear Chills too.

I don't think he's ever had a right job in his life, Brian my other brother is similar to Tone, but he has short brown hair and is about 40 pounds heavier than him, he looks like Gerard Butler with his new style of beard.

'Here, Tony, have you got $20 so I can give it to the guard for more time?'

'Yeah, sure, here you are, Sean.

I beckoned to the guard; can I have ten more minutes as I hand him the $20 note.

'Ok, Mr Sean, but only ten more minutes, cheers.' 'So, Sean, what like is it in here, are you and Phil the only Westerners in here?

(Freedom is the most precious thing you have, till someone takes it away from you) 'Yes we are, but we have a good friend, he's the chief guard in here, his name is Rahul. He took the other ring Phil had, so, we have an easy time here, that's why we have to wear these black armbands.

'That was my next question, why are you wearing the armbands, but now I know.'

'But life is hard in here, the place is very dirty, and there are murders being committed all the time. Two days ago while

I was speaking to Adentric, a guy was shot, that was standing next to me, and his brain matter was splattered all over my fecking face. It was in my hair, everywhere, lucky my mouth was closed at the time. This place is a total fucking nightmare, do you remember that actual film about the American guy that was caught with all that hashish in turkey, Midnight Expresso or it's something like that, well this jail is ten (10) time worse than that, it's a total nightmare. So many things happen here every day, your mind is always playing catch up with your eyes. I have seen more dead people in here than a fecking undertaker and we are in it, but we will survive, you have to learn what you see here you did not see, this place is over run with drugs and deadly violence, you can't let your guard down for one minute here. To survive in here you have to show respect to your fellow in-mates, if you don't do that then you are a dead man walking, this place is not like the jails back home, there are about three TVs in here, no gym, the prisoners use a pole about 5 feet long, with empty 2 lt water-bottles filled with sand as a weight lifting bar, and shortened poles as dumbbells. This place can turn people in to monsters, *"wink, wink"*

You see no evil, speak no evil, and hear no evil; you will survive by that code.

'Well, you have to survive, don't let the place grind you down Sean, and tell Phil the same.

'Ok, will do.

Can you give me your I-phone because I have only got a regular phone, and when you get home, can you top it up with lots of credit?

Yeah sure Sean, here take my I-phone.

Cheers Brian, take out your sim card, and I will put in my one, and I want to send you some picture text messages, of two stone tablets and a photo of a drinking vessel, can you print out a few copies of each item, and send them in with the books?

Yeah, sure, I can do that for you, Sean.

I see them now, is that why you want the book about hieroglyphs.

'Time is up, Mr Sean.' The cell guard said, almost screaming.

'See you all soon, brothers, tell everybody we were asking for them, and don't say anything about the escape.

'What escape, Sean?' 'Nice one, bros.' 'Here, how's notchie-boy?' 'He keeps on looking at the door waiting for you to walk through it.

'I will be back sooner or later, fingers-crossed.' 'We are all waiting for that day to come, our lips will be sealed.' 'Good, remember to say nothing to nobody.

I was reading about this prison Sean, and Amnesty International says, this prison dehumanises the Prisoners, death is an everyday occurrence, people getting stabbed, murdered. Once a prisoner was killed and covered with a blanket he was only discovered two weeks after he went missing, 'Sean forgot to tell you; you remember you worked with Ozzi Mcpliers' 'Yeah sure, I do, I worked with him last year, why?'

'Well, he handed in his laptop into the repair shop, and they found thousands of indecent pictures of children and videos, he's on the run the police think he's left the country on a fake passport. The High Court trial went ahead without him and the Judge said it was one of the worst cases' of child abuse that has ever come before him. All of the jury were excused from further jury duty, most of the women on the jury were crying after seeing the videos and pictures of him sexually abusing children. The judge sentenced him to eight (8) life sentenced in his absence. He's some sick bastard, Mc pliers is. He was on his computer at home, paying a family in the Philippines to sexually abuse their four young children and watching them doing it on the internet. People like that are not fit to walk this earth.

'You are not joking there, bro, hope they catch him before he attacks another child.

And there was more of them in Dundee, two trade union officials, Helen Abramsson, and her boyfriend Jimmy Ackermann, he was in charge of going around all the schools in Tayside checking all the lights, but what the police found was that he was installing little video camaras, in the lights of all the toilets, and changing rooms, and the shower rooms, filming all the children getting undressed, and in the showers, and even when the children were on the toilets. He was live streaming the children on the dark-web. They had thousands of followers world-wide paying money to watch the live streams. He denied any wrongdoing, but the police found his finger prints on the tiny camaras as well as Helen Abramsson's prints as well. She was buying them on an inter-net site and giving them to Jimmy Ackermann, to do his dirty deeds. They were running everything from the new trade union offices in Dundee, they had to get offices on the ground floor because Helen, could not walk up the three flights of stairs. She says that her medical condition she has, has made her put on body weight, that's a load of shit. I was at a seminar last year, she was there as well, the guy holding the seminar was telling the 30 people there that lunch was provided. Sandwiches and pizzas were delivered to the next room, lunch break will be in 15 minutes. Helen excused herself, saying she had to go to the toilet. Come lunch time, she was already in the room eating all the food, she's a big fat greedy bastard, and another thing it took the police three month working shifts, to go through all the material they were all given life sentences.

'Time is up, Mr Sean.

The other members of the paedophile ring were rounded up : 30 in the UK, and 200 more world-wide, Ozzi Mcpliers also had indicated transsexual pornography.

Later in the cell with Phil.

'Here, Phil, my bro's were asking for you and told you to keep your chin up.' 'Cool, did you give them the ring to sell?' 'Course I did Phil, so let's lay the foundation for our escape, good, now we need Nikki on board for this all to happen.' 'When is she writing to you, Phil?' 'She's not, she's coming here to visit tomorrow.' 'Good, let's hope she likes you.' 'Yeah, she will.

'Mr Sean, no female, can resist me once I put on my charm.

'Yeah, that's why you're still pulling the head off it Phil.' 'Phil, do you think your Alfresco of Narcissus, you have to love other people than yourself Phil.' 'ok, Mr Sean stop going on about it, anyway who is Alfresco of Narcissus?' 'I will tell you later Phil.' 'Cheers Mr Sean, for your vote of confidence anyway.' 'It's an open visit; let's hope everything goes well, Phil.

I got my brother's I-phone, do you remember Pablo's priest's second name?

Sure, do Mr Sean, Murphy, Father Mackie Murphy why?

Well, I did some checking up on the internet via the I phone, and Father Mackie Murphy, was killed in a car crash while in Rome, he had been summoned back to see the Pope, and guest what.

Go on then, Mr Sean, tell me?

When the Polizia di Stato (*Italian police force*) *and the ambulance came, they found, Father Murphy seated in his car, with his throat ripped out, and his heart was missing.'*

I see Mr Sean so Father Mackie was going to see the Pope, must be to tell him about Pablo and the werewolves and vampires, but they killed him first.'

Spot on Phil, and the picture of Father Mackie Murphy, on the internet, is the same priest that lives with Pablo Escobar and his family, so Pablo cloned him. Remember Pablo saying he had his scientists clone his pet dogs from his childhood, and the animals as well in his nature reserve, well he's cloning people as well, he's far too advanced for our time Phil. Remember Dolly the Scottish sheep? Scientists cloned her in 2003 from an adult somatic cell, using the process of nuclear transfer.' How do you ken about all that, Mr Sean? Because I read about it in the science Magazine on the plane coming over here.'

That was handy, Mr Sean, or should I call you Einstein.

That how you get educated, by reading the books, not by getting stoned and drinking beer.

I was reading an article about Dolphins on the plane coming over here too; It was saying Dolphins are the cleverest mammals in the oceans, how do they work that one out Mr. Sean?

Well, Phil, you never hear of a fisherman catching a Dolphin now, do you? Sure they catch other fish, sharks, Barracuda, Tuna, but never a Dolphin. If whales were clever like a Dolphin they would resurface at the back of the Japanese whaling ships, and none of them who have gotten killed for so call scientific purposes, ok mate that's how they are intelligent, well in my book anyway mate.

I suppose your right, but I've no smoked any grass in about.

Yeah Phil in about four days, that how we are here, because of you smoking that shit and hitting on Pablo's fecking daughter, anyway that's water under the bridge, but Phil why is Pablo cloning people? He must have some advanced technology from the drinking vessel or something else they found In the cave?

Dinnae ask me Mr Sean because I dinnae ken.

Yeah, Phil, I know you dinnae ken, it just a figure of speech, it sounds funny you talking Dundonian when everybody else is speaking English, remember if you talk like that here They will not have a clue what you are talking about, you will have to pronounce your words and talk slower, mate. Yes, I know that Mr Sean, this is getting like some Hollywood movie, this shit should not be happening to two guys from Dundee.'

Well it is Phil, and we will just have to ride it out and see where it all ends up mate, I have been checking up on my phone how to kill *vampires*.

Really, Mr Sean, you don't believe in all that what you read on the internet.

Phil, it's our only hope mate, listen to this,

1. Decapitation and stuff the severed head of *vampire* with garlic.
2. A wooden stake through the heart.
3. Too much sunlight.

Mr Sean, is that not just killing a *vampire*, like the ones in the films?

Yes, Phil, I am just looking to see if I can pick up anything that's all mate.

Does it say anything about holy water Mr Sean?

That's it, Phil, you did it,

Did what Mr Sean?

That's what the ancient Aliens are afraid of, Phil,

Your speaking with a forked tongue?

They are afraid of holy water, remember I said something was missing at the Cathedral in Pablo's Grounds, well there was no holy water in the font at the entrance of the Cathedral, because remember when we entered the Cathedral, we put our fingers in the font to bless ourselves with the holy water, but it was dry?

You're right Mr Sean, the holy water must kill them or do something to them, that's why they're afraid of it, but remember one thing, Mr Sean, where do we get holy water from in here?

We will work something out, Phil; I am not coming this far to give up now.

Five days later the book came by express delivery. Here Phil, the print of the tablets and drinking vessel has come, here they are. You will have to keep them with you all the time. If you get anything from them, tell me, asap Phil, ok.

Yeah sure will do Mr Sean, but I may not get anything through but will keep them with me all the time and sleep with them close to my body Mr Sean.

Do what you must do, Phil.

Next morning, any news Phil.

nothing Mr Sean, I can't summon it up any time I want, if I could, I would have my show on the Las Vegas strip in America, we will just have to wait for it big boy, can you give me $20.'

Why are you going to buy some Colombian grass with it, Phil?

No, a new prison guard is selling dippers mate.'

Well, Phil, are you going to tell me what a dipper is?

Yeah sure, it's a cigarette dipped in *"PCP"* I want to be zooted/lunched *out, means to be intoxicated on "PCP."*

Phil, you have to keep your head clear of any drugs mate. This is the time we need your sixth sense more than ever, you start taking *"PCP,"* you are signing your own death warrant, so the answer is no fecking way mate, there is no other substance on earth that motivates evil in people than *"PCP."'*

How tae hell do you know all this Mr Sean or should I call you *Quincy M.E.*

I have seen a program about "PCP" on TV. This black American guy was walking down the street in Ohio Cleveland, no clothes on totally out his head on "PCP," and his lower stomach was cut open and his guts were hanging out, obviously cause by self-mutilation. The paramedics came and took the guy to hospital, and this police officer got interviewed. He was saying while out on patrol, he was flagged down by a female in the nude, high on PCP, saying she had slit the throats of her four young children. Yhe oldest was eight years old, and the youngest was six months old and set fire to the house when the policeman went to her house, sure enough, the house was ablaze, the fire crew found the children in the living room with their throats cut. Phil that stuff cause the worst mental illness ever *schizophrenia,* and I can ensure you *schizophrenia* not only affects the person but all his family and people close to them as well Phil and you are not sharing the cell with me, cause I am not watching you for 12 hours, high as a kite, and hallucinating thinking you are going to cut my throat, no fecking way Phil.'

Mr Sean, I would never do that to you, mate.

Phil, I know you know you wouldn't do it, but do you think that woman woke up in the morning saying to herself I am going to get high as fuck kill my children and set fire to my house? Course, not *"PCP"* changes your brain chemistry, and sometimes not for the good mate, people kill other people on that shit mate, so you're not riding the big dipper on our money mate, no fecking way. I was talking to a medical student *Kevin Barry. He* was studying the effects of *"PCP"* on the mind for his Ph.D. qualification; he was telling me this as well, Phil does Rahul know this guy selling *"PCP"* in his jail.

I don't know, but guess you're right, I will not take any drugs again, well not until I get some readings through.'

That's the way to do it. Phil keep your head cleared, and once we get out of here, you can do anything you want to do, mate, ok. *The prison guard was paid off that day after I told Rahul.*

211

We had to wait 26 days later until Phil had some good news, Mr Sean, Mr Sean, wake up I've seen everything, it was just like a movie.'

Morning Phil that great, give me time to wake up and tell me everything you had seen.'

The *werewolves and vampires* come from a planet called Winpoo. Winpoo was an Ancient world, a frozen wasteland frozen in time, it once had two suns orbit the planet, but the suns had died out. It was about to be ripped apart in the death rows, until the *werewolves and vampires* landed there and regenerated the suns with the help of Machetwa. Winpoo is billions of light-years away from Earth, the *werewolves and vampires* then turned on each other, they were mortal enemies for thousands of years,

Until one day their planet was attacked by the *Goomons,* these *Goomons,* are space Pirates of the galaxies and solar systems, and remember they are billions of solar systems out there in space. They look like *Cyclopes, from Greek mythology,* they have a massive body size, are about eight feet tall, and will eat anything that moves they are savages, the most fearsome warriors out there, with superpowers, beams of rays producing from their eye, disintegrates anything the Goomons focus on. They also fly, what I can only describe as *Dragons,* even these *Dragons* have super powers, not only breathing flames, they spray some liquid that melts anything it comes in to contact with, and if one of the *Goomons* die or get killed, they duplicate ten times over, there are millions of these monsters and millions of *vampires* and *werewolves* on planet Winpoo, all in constant battles with each other. Much like the Roman gladiators, here on earth fighting to the death. The planet Winpoo is about ten times the size of Earth, same atmosphere here on earth, mountains, oceans, very large forests, this is where the *werewolves and the vampires* like to fight the *Goomons* in the forests, only because the *Goomons* find it very difficult to manoeuvre and fly their *Dragons* through the forests. These *Goomons* have other life forms on Winpoo, taken from other planets, but they are kept like wild animals, as humans do on Earth zoo's. Massive zoo's the size of the African continent 40 million km, but the zoos are really for breading the aliens, just like farmers do here on Earth. Now Mr Sean lets be sure we understand the dangers of these creatures from outer space, the *werewolves and vampires* are as real as me and you, they never came to Earth to study humans, because they are humans on Winpoo as well stolen from Earth since the dawn of time, people from Earth was the food for the *werewolves and vampires*. Millions of humans been bred like cattle here on Earth, millions have died at the hands of the Aliens, now when the *Goomons* came the only species they don't eat is humans, they are now the servants of the *Goomons*, nothing can stop them, but once Pablo has and puts the other pieces together, who knows Mr Sean, who knows, the *Goomons* have like contests like the Romans did all those years ago, Alien life forms, fighting like gladiators fighting for survival, and to win their freedom, machetwa has god-like powers to the holder. Still, it affects the *Goomons* because it can't penetrate the force field surrounding them and the *Dragons.*

Why do they not like eating humans, Phil?

I don't know, and I never picked up why they don't like eating humans.

So, it's just like jungle warfare, let the enemy come to you fighting in your terrain?

That's precisely what the ancient Aliens are doing to the *Goomons,* they are constantly flying over the jungles, and the *Dragons* are setting fire to the woodlands. Spraying acid-like vapor over everything and destroying all the vegetation it comes into contact with, trying to get at the *werewolves and vampires,* these jungles are like thousands of square miles, and the *werewolves and vampires* have tunnels like an underground city linking to all the other tunnels.

The Goomons have no conscience they just destroy.

The *Goomons* are hunters, they are looking for food, and the other species in all the different galaxies and solar systems are on the main menu. Still, if the *werewolves and vampires* enter Earth's solar system, the milky way, then every living being will be on the menu, including humans, they can easily take Earth in a matter of weeks if not days, Mr Sean.

So why are the *werewolves and vampires* here, why travel billions of miles through space to come to earth?

I believe it is all to do with *machetwa*, that is what the drinking vessels called, it has miraculous powers. How can I say this? It is the equivalent to the holy grail here on Earth, human and alien life cannot comprehend the capabilities of machetwa; is only working about 10% of its full power, there are four stone like diamonds that will have to be inserted into *machetwa*, two slots into the front, one slot into the back of it and one slot into the base; and then, only then will the holder have full powers of *machetwa, the werewolves and vampires* are hiding the machetwa from the *Goomons*.

So, if the *werewolves and vampires,* and the *Goomons* come here to Earth, there will be three Alien species fighting on Earth for machetwa with humans in the middle? We are going to get wiped out.

Phil that is why Pablo is paying the Peruvian government all they $billions, to excavate Machu Picchu, he knows that the Diamond stones are in the spacecraft under Machu Picchu; they must have found something else in the cave where machetwa was taken from, some written scripture, Phil it has to be the hieroglyphs stone slabs, but what has Egyptian hieroglyphs got to do with everything that's going on here?

Mr Sean, they have been to Earth before the ancient Aliens if they helped the Inca people with the technology to build Machu Picchu, why not the great pyramids in Giza.'

Nevertheless, Phil, why travel billions of miles through space, to here on Earth.'

That is the good news mate, they are Billions of light-years away from Earth, but the bad news is that it took them two months to travel here. They go through time by a vast network of wormholes, they are links to every universe every Galaxy, and every solar system, but remember there are Billions of these wormholes out there in open space. Man will never discover the true meaning of them, well not for a long time. Mr Sean I am away to have asleep as I have been up all night, watching all this being played out in my head.

This is unbelievable Phil I cannot comprehend the situation we are in. What are the chances of all this happening here on Earth, not Billions but Trillions to one mate, and if the *Goomons* come here looking for the *machetwa* Earth is no more; the human race will be wiped out in a matter of days. Do not tell anyone about this Phil, ok mate.'

Yes, I do know the routine, but the chances of the *Goomons* coming here are hundreds of Billions to one Mr Sean, I am away to sleep for a while now good night, or should I say good day.'

Yes, Phil, I will let you get some sleep I am away to see what is happening in the prison yard, but remember Phil there is always a chance, seeya.

Next day11.15 am, visiting time, Phil had gone to see Nikki while I am waiting in the cell for Phil to come back.' 'Hey, Mr Sean.' 'Phil, how did it go?' 'Let us say I am in love, and she is very beautiful 'That is good for you, Phil, I am happy for you.'

'Is she coming back here to see you?' 'Yes, she will be back in the next couple of days. Here are some cakes she baked for the both of us, she is away to hand in some cakes to the guards as well. You have been away for about two hours, were you telling her your life story? I thought something had happened.' 'It was not a private visit Mr Sean, we had to go into the hall with about 40 other inmates and their families. If you were lucky and there on time, you got a chair and table, if not, you had to stand speaking to your visitors. The chairs and tables are falling apart, like everything else in this shit hole of jail and the smell of the people with all the heat in here was very potent, I will not go into detail about what we were talking about, but she is very interested in me.'

'Cool, Phil, you have to keep her sweet, you will have to wait and gain her trust but do not say anything about escaping from here, wait till about a couple of weeks before you tell her.'

'How can I tell her anything, Mr Sean?' 'I do not know the plan myself.' 'Phil, I am still planning it out, but do not worry, you will be the first to know.'

I sat up on the bed, thinking to myself. Seven days have passed since my brothers went home, I will phone Dad in the morning.

Morning of the next day. 'Hello Dad, Sean here.' 'How are you keeping, son?' 'Good Dad, did you find a buyer for the ring?'

'Well Sean, the twins (the twins are two brothers that deal in antiquities, in Dundee Scotland) have a buyer for the ring.' 'Well, dad, how much the buyer willing to pay?' '£2,000,000,000.'

'"Fuck sake two million pounds" 'Sean, that's cash in hand, the twins have taken off their seller's fee 'That is brilliant, cannot wait to tell Phil.' 'Sean, I will have the money in a couple of days.

'Sure, Dad, I will phone you, later, love to all Dad.' 'Take care Sean and watch yourself in there, I have been looking at the prison on the internet, and it does not look like an amicable place especially for Westerners.'

'Yes, Dad, but we are ok, we are good friends with the main guard here, and nobody gives Phil or me any trouble at all.' 'That is good Sean but watch yourself ok.' 'Yeah sure, talk soon bye.'

'Phil, Phil, guess what?'

'You dug a tunnel.' 'Ha-ha, no, that ring that cunt Pablo Escobar gave me, my Dad's got two million pound for it.' 'can you say that again Mr Sean?' 'Phil, this is going to help the both of us to get tae feck out of this shit-hole, let us go for a walk in the yard.'

The yard was full of people most days, just lying about taking their drugs, escaping from reality. The yard was where most of the murders and stabbings happen and people getting their throats cut, so it was not a safe place, especially if you are a gringo.

Nevertheless, we had Rahul on our side, and everybody respected him because the other men say his favourite punishment was that the person had to stand on a chair in the punishment cell with his hands tied behind his back. A pulley lifted their arms, that was bolted on the roof and secured on to the doubled winged bracket that was located in the middle of the side-wall until the person felt the tension; he had to stand there on the chair until he collapsed, exhausted. This, in turn, dislocates your two arms from the shoulders, most people had to stand days before exhaustion took its toll because it is an excruciating and inhumane way of torture.

That was a favourite way of torture in the Nazi death camps, 50,000 people endured this torture in Auschwitz alone between 1940-1945, once they endured the torture, most of them were gassed soon after collapsing exhausted.

In the yard of the jail, there were pieces of string used as a clothesline, but most of the clothes on the lines were all holed and tattered just like rags people use to clean their shoes with, but to the people in here, this was the way they lived. *Moreover, you think you have it hard.*

Everybody was talking to Phil and myself only because we had the black armbands, and everybody was fearful of Rahul.

I was asking who the big guy was wearing the baseball cap, one of the inmate's replied. 'He is Samson; he is Rahul's enforcer, he carries out some of the beatings, he used to be in the Columbian special forces, Mr Sean.'

'Yeah, sure he was, he must have been "a fucking roadblock then" He has got more chins than a Chinese phone book, he must be about 370 lb, a big lump of a guy who ate all the pies.

'Sorry, Mr Sean, I do not understand.'

'It is a song back home in Scotland, about people being overweight.'

'Please sing it, Mr Sean, I would like to hear it.'

'Ok, then sure.'

'Sing along all together now,

who ate all the pies,

who ate all the pies,

you fat bastard, you fat bastard,

you ate all the pies,

you ate all the pies,

who ate all the pies,

you fat bastard, you fat bastard

you ate all the piessssssssssssss.

'Mr Sean, do not let him hear you say that about him.'
'Why will he sit on me?' 'Mr Sean, he will take great umbrage
to that.'

Fifty-five years in this place is going to be a fecking
nightmare, and we have only been here 40 days, Mr Sean.'

Do not worry about it, Phil, only 202,900 days to go, mate,
our day will come, so dinnae worry about it keep yourself
focused Phil. Everybody at sometime in their lives fucks up,
but you did it big time Phil. You really went for it didn't you;
I am away to see Adentric, 'to see if he can get a saxophone in
here and a pair of binoculars.'

'Ok, Mr Sean, but why do you need binoculars?'

'Well, Phil, you are going to see Rahul and ask him if you
can go on cleaning duty, so you get to the watch-tower looking

over the four corners off the jail.' 'What if he asks why all the interest to go on cleaning the watch-towers.'

'Tell him you liked to watch birds back home in Dundee and that is why you have the binoculars, 'I will tell my brother Tone, when he is sending the books, to include a book about Columbia birds, the feathered type that is.'

'I see Mr Sean, let us hope he believes me.' 'Sure, he will, you are his golden blue-eyed boy Phil, and if he does not believe you, well, you will have to suck him off.' 'F*ck that Mr Sean, I am not going to do that, no fecking way.'

'Ha ha ha, I am only pulling your leg, Phil, chill-axe, I am sure everything will be okay, here is Adentric now.

'Buen dia, zeb, un dia encantador Mr Sean, Phil, seria mejor si estuvieramos en el exterior.

'El seria el senor Adentric.

'I see you are learning Spanish, Mr Sean, that is very good, but nearly everybody in Columbia speaks English.

'Yes, Adentric, but I will be here for a very l-o-n-g time.' 'You sure will be Mr Sean.

'I will only be here a matter of months, three months to be exact.' 'Lucky you Adentric, Phil and I will be in here for years and years.' 'I know Mr Sean, and it must be hard realizing you will be in here for 55 years.

Rub it in, why don't you Adentric, a**hole.

'Adentric, I would like to place an order for a saxophone.'
'Sure, Mr Sean, I can get you one, it has to be a soprano saxophone for playing the blues.'

'Sure, thing Mr Sean, no-problemo.'

'And one more thing, would it be possible for you to bring a laptop in?'

'Yes, Mr Sean, I can get you anything you wish here, Mr Sean, Phil.'

'Can you get me a helicopter to land in the yard and to fly the both of us out of here, Adentric?'

'You are very funny, Phil, I am so sorry I cannot get you one, Phil.'

'Adentric, that was not a joke that was a serious request, one more request, I would like you to bring me an internet-stick as well.'

'of course, the price will be a mere $1,350, and sorry, Mr Sean, but you will have to give cash up front.'

'Wait here, Adentric, and I will return with the money.'

Phil and I went back to the cell. 'Phil, give me the padlock key, *you have to keep your bar cell door padlocked at all times, or someone would be in your cell stealing all your goods and money, even here in the top cell landing, people and guards would steal from you.'*

224

We quickly went back to meet Adentric after we got what we needed from our cell.

Adentric looks up at Phil and tries to read his expression as he talks. 'How did you like my sister Phil? did you like her, yes?'

'Yeah, your sister knocks the ball out of the park, she is stunningly beautiful.'

'I knew you would like her Phil, never disrespect Nikki, she is the only family I have here in Columbia.'

'Here you are, Adentric, $1,350, all in crisped $100 notes.' 'Thank you very much Mr Sean, it may take 4-5 days, we would like to hear you playing your saxophone.'

'Sure, thing Adentric, maybe be in a few months, I can play to everybody in here, the main guards in here, Ortega, Diego, Alejangom Santiago, they all like the blues.'

This place is so hot in here, all day and all night, never a chilly day in the yard. To the side, there is a shower, well it is supposed to be a shower, the water was foul and unhygienic, nearly everybody that uses the shower suffers from diarrhoea diseases, guinea worm, diseases, *typhoid, and dysentery. If the guards do not kill you or the other prisoners, the water will kill* you; *we were far better off than the other people in the jail, being on the top landing, a prisoner here is well* looked after, *only because he has money to pay the guards with (well that is not true, it is because of Rahul and the ring that he stole from Phil that keeps us from living like animals).*

There was a child sized paddling pool, at the north wall in the yard I am curious, why it was in here, but the next day I found out why it was there. A child rapist has just been sentenced to 15 years in jail, as soon as he came back from the court, the inmates grabbed him, and his head was held under the water, till he died. The prison guards were watching and never interfered, he got Columbian justice from the prisoners.

(DEJA VU)

'Mr Sean, I have spoken to Rahul about cleaning the watchtower and the and the guard's mess room, and what did he say, Phil?'

'I am just going to tell you, Mr Sean, he looked at me and said, "I hope you are not planning to escape from here, because if you do there's a bullet with your name on it, Phil," pointing his finger in my face, smiling, 'Phil, you do not worry about the bullet with your name on it, you worry about the bullet with "to whom it may concern on it!"

'He just laughed and smiled, and said, why of course I can, I did explain to him about bird watching, and he said the south tower would be better because it is only 15 feet away from the jungle – a lush, tropical background. It is funny because the north side of the prison was only 10 feet away from the city, and about 20 minutes' walk away from the centre of town.

'Nice one, Phil, are you not going to tell me the plan of escape then Mr Sean?'

'Yes, in a few days' time Phil.' 'Phil, you will be the first to know.'

'Ha ha ha, Mr Sean, who else are you going to tell?'

***

'Mr Sean, I have got your saxophone and laptop.' 'Great Adentric.'

Adentric is a nice guy, he stands about 6'2 high and is quite muscular, and he has a Mohawk hair-cut, that made him look more prominent and meaner. Most people respected him and no doubt they like his beautiful sister as well, there is a lot of the prisoners giving Phil angry looks all because she was visiting him now, and now believe they are giving them to me as well, 'Remember I downloaded all the information from Maria's computer.'

'Yes, Mr Sean, well, I know how Pablo Escobar runs his drug empire, it is all on the memory stick, remember level 5 in Pablo's mansion.'

'Well, that was where all the cocaine comes into by submarines. He has got thirty (30) of the most significant submarines in the world. They pick up all the cocaine in the Americas and bring it by tunnels into level 5 where it's then distributed to the seven continents of the world, Africa, Asia, Australia/Oceania, Europe, North America, and South

America. I have all the information, and come here and see this on my computer in the cell, this is a live feed as it happens, look at the people moving the bales of cocaine. I have been watching this for a few days now. Look at the top left hand side of the screen, there's one of Pablo's men driving a forklift, with four bales of cocaine on a pallet say about 250 lb. He drives the forklift into the chamber, waits about 5 minutes, then goes back into the chamber, and takes out two pallets. This continues all day every day. That chamber it duplicates the cocaine. So from 1 ton of cocaine he's making 100,000 tonnes of cocaine, every fecking day except the weekends, he must rest his machine. Phil, that's how he's making so much money, he just keeps on duplicating 1 ton of cocaine, and he has hundreds of people working there, and there are hundreds of bale of cocaine waiting to be shipped out. There's like a subway leading in to level five, I watch the people coming and going all day long.

Level five is 200 square meters in size, about ten times the size of a football field and this information is going to cripple Pablo's Olmec cartel. We do have the map of all Pablo's hideouts in the Americas and all the pickup points worldwide and the drop of points, as well as every piece of information to bring the Olmec cartel to its knees. Every submarine has a crew of 30 men working on them and the subs doing the long haul shipments take 60 tons of the purest Columbian snow, and at $75.000 per kilo and remember, he has thirty submarines coming and going every week at any one time, there is about $15 billion worth of cocaine in the seas and oceans around the world, that is how the cocaine epidemic has gripped the world. Every town, every city in every country in the world has a "Columbian snow" epidemic, and it is all down to the Olmec cartel, that is how Pablo "fucking" Escobar is the richest man that has ever walked the earth. He is worth £ three thousand billion or $ five thousand billion, he does not count in millions, he counts in billions, and that is what makes him a trillionaire, and Phil Pablo has photos of all his cartel members world-wide and look who is head of the UK operation.'

Yeah, Mr Sean, I do remember seeing them before, but where?

Do remember the two guys from Dundee that started up their pizza shops?

Sure do, but no way is that them?

Angus and Ethan, it is all coming together now, that is how they are dealing their cocaine, their pizza shops are just a front. It all makes sense now who is going to think a pizza shop is selling cocaine, and they are selling it big time, by the kilo's, the pair of them must have 85% of the cocaine trade in the UK, and we are talking £ billions. I was reading somewhere that the cocaine trade in London alone was £2 bn per year and rising, and just imagine how much money the pair of them are making. They are selling pure cocaine uncut from Colombia. No doubt somewhere down the line it will get cut with baking soda or talcum powder, but it will still be 75% pure cocaine getting the user addicted. The better the hit, the more that person will want it, and can guarantee this Angus will be the leading supplier to all the actors In the UK and all the A list of stars will be snorting or smoking the best cocaine in the world thanks to Angus and Ethan.'

You would never believe the pair of them are number one cocaine dealers in the UK, they seem such nice guys. I have never heard of them talking about drugs, and never have they said a bad word about anybody Mr Sean.

That is the way they do it, and they never draw attention to themselves that's what makes them the number one cocaine dealers in the UK, they are the *Apex cartel*, remember about the murders in Dundee, *hatchet, and weasel,?*

course I do mate, things like that dinnae happen every day in Dundee do they, big boy.

Phil do not call me big boy especial in here mate people might take it the wrong way mate ok, now pay attention Phil. While you have been smoking that Colombian grass with the other prisoners I have been checking out everything that's been happening back home via the mobile phone internet connection; now this is going to hit more than that Colombian weed you have been smoking try and focus on what am saying ok mate; yeah sure Mr Sean.

Right, back home in Dundee, and Scotland, there have been ten murders. All of them have drug connections to the underworld, everybody was murdered in the same way. Two bodies been found together in big barrels, mutilated. Their genitals cut off and put into their mouths, and each body has had 66 nails embedded into their heads. So that is ten bodies with 66 nails embedded into their heads, right so 10x66 =666 so Phil what does the number 666 represent?

I have got it too mate, 666 represent 999 upside down Mr Sean; knew you were going to say that Phil everything is a big joke to oneself mate.

Sorry mate, I am a bit stoned right now, but please continue mate.

I wish you would give smoking that weed a break mate, now 666 represents the number of the *BEAST*.

No way, Mr Sean, are you saying the *BEAST* killed them, but why is *Jimmy Savile* killing drug dealers?

No *Jimmy Savile* was accused of being a Paedophile *beast*, not that sort of *BEAST, BUT THE BEAST, BEAST,* the fallen angel the *DEVIL* himself, *SATAN, LUCIFER, DIABLO,* the clue is in the name *YAN YING'S PING'S PIZZA*. They are 18 letters in the title, now 18 divided by 3 = 6, now three sixes are equal the number 666, the number of the *BEAST*.

Mr Sean, I see one small problem, the *DEVIL* has been around far longer than the pizza shops do you not agree with that mate?

Yes, I do Phil, all am saying is the *APEX CARTEL* is Pablo Escobar, as are all the cartels' world-Wide Maybe, just maybe, Pablo is the *DEVIL*, from a different world and the *werewolves* and *vampires* are his foot soldiers; remember Pablo was talking about his dinosaur collection. He said he had seen them as they lived millions of years ago, do you remember him saying that Phil?

Sorry, Cannae remember him saying that mate, as I said, I am stoned.

You said you were keeping off that shit, anyway, mate he did, so everything goes back to that spaceship. Pablo's *machetwa* has given him powers far more advanced than anything here on earth if not the Solar system as we know it; once Pablo has the other pieces for the *machetwa*, his powers will be unbelievable, that is why the Goomons are after it, Philippe.'

Do not call me "Philippe" again, Mr Sean, that is what that transgender freak called me. So you are saying you think cuntae Baz Pablo could travel through time backward and forwards?

Yes that is clearly what I am saying, he can clone animals, he can clone people, and can, and does duplicate, 1 ton of pearly cocaine 94% pure into 100,000 tons of cocaine per day; so why not time travel, he did say that he has seen the dinosaurs in real life, he did say that he can do more than any other human being on earth.

You have got a tremendous sixth sense Phil. I have never met anybody that can do what you can do mate, but you have got a memory like a fish. One thing has been bothering me, Phil, do you remember when I was telling you about the gas chamber operator at the Treblinka death camp in Poland?

Yes, course I do, mate, why?

What was the guy's name again?

Ivon John Demjanjuk why?

How come you can remember his name; it is not like a familiar name you hear in Dundee now.

Because an old man that lived next door to my great granny Grant, that lived up the Lochee road, that was his name Ivon John Demjanjuk he used to tell me stories while I was visiting my gran. He was from Hungary.'

Moreover, one more thing, Phil, how many days have you not smoked some of that weed, while we have been here in Colombia?

Well, I never smoked it when we were in the holding cell, but I did bring a half quarter of rocky, I cut it up into small pieces and, as you say, suitcased it.

So where did you get the rest of it while we were at Pablo's place?

Behind the waterfall in the woods. As you would say I sniffed it out like a truffle pig; I watched Pablo go there and pick some weed off the bushes; it must be for his usage.

Do you remember the manager of the night club back in London, Tony Rogers? Well Pablo had his Sicarios kill him because he stole diamonds from his watch, had just remembered it there as we were talking?

'How do you know that Mr Sean? 'Well he told me when he was talking about his shrunken-heads furthermore, when he offered me £13 million to kill you.'

'If that bastard Pablo were standing here, I would kill the son of a bitch.'

'Phil, the black book says, 'be not overcome with evil but overcome evil with good, Pablo Escobar and the Olmec cartel are the Achilles heel of the drug trade worldwide, once we escape and make it back home, I swear we will bring down the Olmec cartel, and that "cunt" Pablo Escobar.'

***

Two months later

'Mr Sean, Nikki would like to discuss the escape plan with you again, just to make sure she knows every little detail, and she has the passport photos you asked for, to get her the fake passport. She is looking forward to her new life in Dundee, Scotland with me as her husband.'

'Sure Phil, the World Cup kicks off in fourteen (14) days here in Columbia.' 'Right, Mr Sean, she'll be here tomorrow.' 'Good Phil, the last re-run and then all systems go. Remember to tell Nikki to bring her holy-water.'

Why do you want, holy-water, Mr Sean?

Sorry, Phil, forgot to tell you mate, with the holy water, I am going to soak the acid tablets in the sacred water, then give the book with the acid tablets in it back to Nikki. Then I will tell her to put two tablets in per cake; that way we will know how many of the *vampires and werewolves* are in this place, and see what effects the holy-water has on them, if any. Still, it must have some impact on them right, Phil.'

Cool Mr Sean, fingers crossed.

The following day. 'Morning Nikki, you are looking lovely, as you do every day.'

'Why thank you, Mr Sean, here are my passport photos.' 'Good, the fake passports will be here for making our way back home to Scotland. We escape on semi-final day, the 14th July.'

'Here is the book with the black micro-dot acid-tablets.' 'You go home and bake 200 cupcakes, and in the cupcakes, you put in two acid tablets per cup-cake. Then, and remember this, 30 minutes before the kick off, you will hand in the cakes to the prison guards, and tell them they are for the guards watching the football. At half-time, the acid will be taking effect, they will be so much tripping out of their heads, they will not know what is going on. Phil and I will make our way to the south-east watch-tower; the tower will not be manned because all the guards will be watching football, and all the prisoners will be listening to the match on the radios that you handed to them last week, all twenty (20) radios. Once we are in the watch-tower, we will have to jump the four feet onto the wall, then shimmie along the wall to the telegraph-pole, slide down it, and make our way to the car where you and Adentric will be waiting. Then we will drive to the rendezvous point where we will meet up with my brother who will have all the fake passports that he got made in Dundee. This is where we will split-up and mingle in with the rest of the football supporters, and make our way across the Venezuela border to Caracas, then to the Simon Bolivar international airport for the flight to Germany and from there, we will take the plane back home to Bonnie Dundee. By the time we get to Venezuela, the police authorities will know we have escaped and will be looking out for the four of us at every airport in Columbia. That is why we are going to Venezuela, because the airport in Columbia has facial-recognition-cameras. There are no such cameras like them in Venezuela. One more thing I forgot to mention to Phil, can you bring with you a haversack, with two torches, and two bottles of holy water, two whistles, and a container of pepper. Are you clear on everything you have to do at your end, Nikki?'

'Yes, I am Mr Sean.' 'Adentric will be out of jail in two weeks, he knows everything he has to do as well, Mr Sean, I cannot wait to start my new life with Phil in Scotland.'

'Yes, Nikki, and I cannot wait to get out of this Columbian shit hole of jail as well.'

'Mr Sean, you have a visitor waiting to see you.' 'That is strange, Rahul I do not have any visitors today.'

'Well, you have one now, Mr Sean, best not to keep her waiting. *Keep her waiting, whom could it be?*

'Before you go, Mr Sean, a severe incident happened this morning in the centre of town, a baby boy aged two months along with his six years old sister was kidnapped in the city. The police apprehended the culprit in the woods on the outskirts of town, he was performing a vile sexual act on the young baby boy in the woods. The policemen then discovered the young girl mutilated body in the boot of the car 'the officers showed great restraint when they arrested him; his fingerprints were run through the computer and he was discovered to be Interpol's most wanted sex offender. He was traveling on a fake passport, and is wanted in Scotland for crimes against children. His real name is "Ozzi Mcpliers," is wanted in Scotland where he has escaped justice.'

'That is good news Rahul, glad the police got him, and he is a danger to little boys and girls, will he be extradited to Scotland?'

'No Mr Sean, there is no extradition between Columbia and Scotland, he will appear in courts, today and remanded to this prison in the afternoon, the life expectancy of a paedophile and child murderer here in this prison is about 45 minutes; that is how long it takes for the word to go around the prison, the prisoners will give him Columbian justice as they do with all sex offender here in prison.'

I walked away, shaking my head.

Mr Sean, why do you wrap Sellotape around a budgerigar?

PHIL FOR FECK SAKE NOT NOW MATE, OK.

Why are you shouting at me for Mr Sean? I was going to tell you a joke.

Sorry Phil, but that bastard from Dundee, Ozzi Mcpliers, is here in Colombia. The police have just captured him as he was rapping a two-month-old child, and the bastard, has murderer the child's 6-year-old sister mutilating her body; the young boy is at the hospital now the doctors say he is only 10% surviving the horrendous injuries.

I am so sorry mate, what makes a grown man commit such appalling acts of brutality against a helpless young child? Later, in the afternoon.

'Mr Sean, Mc pliers, is here in prison now, come and watch with me.'

'Sure, will Rahul; I will go and get Phil.'

'Here Phil, come and watch this, that Mc pliers is going to get some justice.'

'Just come and watch as the prisoners drown the nonce, that is him there, he has dyed his hair black and looks he is still wearing his "noncey cuntae metal rim glasses,"

look at the fear on his face, it says it all, payback time, I am going down to the paddling pool Phil, hand me the knife, the prisoners are giving him one hell of a beating.'

'Do not get involved, Mr Sean.'

'I am going to slit his throat and put my foot on his head to keep him under the water, Phil, that is all.'

'Mr Sean, you are turning into the animals in here, mate, that will be etched in your memory forever.'

'Yes I know Phil, but why should he have a quick death, he tortured and mutilated, and the police believe he had eaten some body parts. I am not doing this for myself, but for every child that has been harmed by this monster; every photo and every video that these people look at, they are as guilty as the people that are doing this type of crime against children. So, I think I can live with seeing him breathe in water for the last and only time.'

Well, Mr Sean did you do it to him?

No Phil, the other prisoners, gave him a "Colombian necktie,"

You will have to tell me what is "Colombian necktie"?

They cut his throat, and pulled his tongue out through the gaping wound, and sliced off his ears, but I did put my foot on his head, while he was submerged underwater. I do not know how because he was knocking on deaths door, mate, here is a souvenir from him, *as I tossed Phil Mcpliers left ear.'*

Feck sake Mr Sean why are you giving his bloody ear to me, mate?

Well, you know what they say, Phil, *"ear today, gone tomorrow."*

"The children will be safe now that the nonce is dead."

'Mr Sean, remember your visitor been waiting for 20 minutes now!'

'Maria, what are you doing here? Did you come to visit me? if Pablo finds out, he will kill you and me.'

'That is not true Mr Sean, Pablo would never harm me in any way.' 'Every time I see you, Maria, you look better each time.' 'Thank you, Mr Sean, I have good news.'

'Are we going home?' 'No Mr Sean, yourself and Phil are being transferred to the high-security jail soon.' (*Fucking hell*) … 'That is great, Maria.'

'Do you have a date for this move.' 'Yes, it will be two days after the World Cup semi-final, Mr Sean. I will be able to come and visit you more often there. I am doing my best to get Pablo to pardon yourself and Phil. Given time, he will come around to my way of thinking, and we can be together forever, Mr Sean.'

'Thank you for everything, Maria.

(That is *two days after we go over the wall, we will be transferred*).

'Mr Sean, we will have more privacy in the high-security jail. I will be able to stay the night with you.

'I look forward to the time we will spend together, Maria.'

'I have to go now Mr Sean, goodbye.' As she kisses my lips.

Later, I was alone with Phil. 'Here, Phil, Maria just came to visit, and she says we are getting moved to the high-security jail two days after the semi-finals.'

'But that is two days after we escape, did you tell her about the escape? did you?'

'No way, the only people that know are me and you, Nikki and Adentric.'

'Adentric will be out in 4 days.' 'Cool, Phil, your sister will be here next week to get the passport photos, then she will fly back to Dundee and give them to Tone who will get a fake passport made and bring them out here and hand them over in Venezuela, then it is party time as we are going home.'

***

Two days before semi-finals, Columbia vs. England and Japan v Germany.

"We only have one window of opportunity to escape, and that is the world cup finals."

'Phil, I have spoken to my brother, and everything is good. He will be out here tomorrow with the fake passports. He has booked into the Spero hotel in Venezuela, which is a ten-minute taxi ride to the airport, then check it and homeward bound, this is on the "run day" Phil, Sunday, five (5) hours from now, we will be on our way to freedom with God's speed. Remember, act as normal as possible, this is going to be the biggest day in our lifetime, let us hope everything goes to plan.'

Mr Sean, hope England does not win the world cup because we will never hear the end of it.'

Phil, they still go on about winning it in 1967, mate, so dinnae worry about it.'

Sorry, Mr Sean, but it was 1966. England won the world cup, you are not always wrong, Mr Sean, but you are not always right as well.

So it was Phil *Celtic, the Lisbon Lions,* won the European cup in 1967 the first British team to do so Beating Inter Milan 2-1, but to tell you the truth, Phil, I am not bothered who wins the World Cup just as long as we get out of this place and back home.

The whole of the jail was in a buzz with Columbia being in the semi-final, 15 minutes before kick-off.

'Where the hell is Nikki? she should be here by now with the cakes for the guards, phone her.'

'You have the phone Mr Sean.' 'Nikki, Sean here, where the hell are the pair of you.'

'Sorry, Mr Sean, but we have a flat tyre, and Adentric cannot find the wheel brace to change the wheel.'

'For feck sake, get a taxi, get here any way possible, but you have to be here now.'

'Mr Sean, everybody will be watching Columbia in the semi-finals, there will be no taxi's and all the buses will be off the road until the game is over.'

Five (5) minutes later, before kick-off.

'Looks like we are not going anywhere, Phil.'

The phone suddenly rings in my pocket. Ring-ring- 'Hello Mr Sean, we are here, am just going to bring in the cakes to the jail.' 'Good, did you get a taxi?' 'No, Adentric found the wheel brace under the seat.

'Good Nikki, phone me back once you are out of jail.'

Ten minutes later.

'Mr Sean, I am back out of jail, and the guards are eating the cakes and watching football. We will be parked across the road with our light on, ok Mr Sean.'

***

'*Here we go again we're on the road again,* we will be with you all in 10 minutes.'

Suddenly the jail erupted into cheers, Columbia just scored a goal, 7 minutes before half time, the yard was empty. Everybody is watching the game, all the watchtowers are un-manned.

My plan is like a chain if one link breaks, it all collapses. Have you got the keys to the towers main gate?

'Sure, do Mr Sean.

'Phil, I will be back in 1 minute, I have left my phone in the cell.'

'Hurry up then, Mr Sean; I told you I would only be a minute Phil.'

'Here we go then Phil. The ladder was about 30 feet high once we are at the top, it is only a four-foot jump, and we are just about free, here go's Phil,

"*one small step for man*

one giant leap for Mr Sean."

ahh.'

'Are you ok, Mr Sean?'

'Yes, Phil, I just battered my knees off the wall, best you jump sideways, Phil.'

'Mr Sean, catch this bag, and then it is my turn.' 'No Probs Phil.'

I can't stop my legs from shaking Mr Sean!

For fuck sake Phil I never knew you had a fear of hights?

I dinnae, I have a fear of falling, but here goes big boy.

'That is, it, Phil, we have made it this far, no going back now, we need to shimmie along the wall, then slide down the pole, I will go first Phil.'

Phil and I gradually made our way down the pole as carefully as possible. 'Perfect that we are out of that fecking jail.'

'There are Nikki and Adentric; we are going back to the Badlands.' I said, almost feeling like hugging them.

'We were thinking you were not coming, Mr Sean, Phil. Let's get going. Here are the Columbia football shirts, put them on and hang the Columbia flags out of the window, so people will think we are just supporters, out celebrating like everyone else. And here is the haversack with everything you asked for Mr Sean.

Final score, Columbia- 4, England- 3, it was like the Mardi Gras. The whole of Columbia was out in the streets.

I looked around, carefully observing. 'Feck sake, we are never going to make it across the border at this rate, hundreds and thousands of people were now in the streets of every town, city, and village.'

'We will make it to the border once we get onto the motorway Mr Sean, and then it is 20 miles, to freedom, Mr Sean, Phil.

Meanwhile, at Pablo's super mansion where he is entertaining all of Columbia elite and watching the big game.

'Don Pablo.' 'Yes Maria.'

'There has been a security breach.' 'Do not worry about it, Maria, my sicario's, will take care of it.'

'But Pablo, the breach has come from internal. Someone had copied all the files from your computer that is in my office, there are only two people that can gain access to the computer, myself and Yours truly, nobody can gain access.'

'Mr Sean! He had access, remember when he used the computer to email someone. Mr Sean is the only person that could have done this, he has got all the files! That has every route that the submarines take, every pickup point and every drop-off point, all of the cocaine labs in the Americas and worldwide. This will have grave consequences if the Americans get this information and the w.d.a.a.d (world.

direct. action. against. drugs). Mahmoud, take eight sicario's to the prison and bring Mr Sean and Phil, take the helicopter, you will be there in 20 minutes and call on the phone once you have them, ok............move it !'

Meanwhile, 20 miles away at the other end. Phil and I are struggling to get our asses out of Columbia.

'Mr Sean, we have to stop at the gas station for fuel up ahead, then it is only 5 miles to the border.' Said Adentric.

Nikki turned her head to look at me properly. 'I have to use the lady's room as well, Mr Sean.'

'Ok, quick as you can.'

Meanwhile, back at the jail.

'Pablo, we have landed in jail.' 'And? Yes, Mahmoud.' 'Mr Sean and Phil have escaped; they have somehow killed the guards.' 'what? All of them!'

'Yes, Don Pablo, all of them.' Their uniforms are all lying about the prison, it is like they have all been vaporized into dust, there are piles of dust every were, not prison guards to be seen anywhere, Pablo, Mr Sean and Phil', somehow knew the guards were, *VAMPIRES*.'

If they know that, they will also know about the *WEREWOLVES*, 'I want them found, get every policeman and woman in Columbia, every soldier, we have thousands of *werewolves*, and *vampires*, here in Columbia. I will transmit a message telepathically to my army of *werewolves and vampires.* Put it on the news, the radio, the person that brings me Mr Sean dead or alive, I will give them $100,000,000,000, tell every gang member, I want them found now!'

'Mr Sean, you see all the police and army helicopters in the sky, they have somehow discovered that we have escaped. It will seem they have somehow found out that we have all the information about the drug-routes because no way would all the police and army be searching for two escaped prisoners.'

'Be quiet, Phil, here comes Adentric and Nikki. we will talk about it later, Phil, ok.'

'Mr Sean, it was on the news that there are roadblocks up ahead. I know an old FARC trail that will take everybody to the border. *Meanwhile, Pablo has upped the reward to $150,000,000,* we can dump the car here and walk the rest of the way.'

The trail was over-grown, people have not used this track in years. *The first few miles were easy, but after that my shoes and Phil shoes, started to bite into our heals and sides of our feet. After all, we had only walked about 1 mile per day in jail. The adrenaline is pumping through our bodies, and the heat from the Colombian humidity was causing sweat to run down our faces and into the eyes, so we had to keep on wiping our foreheads to stem the flow of sweat.* We had only walked 5 miles or so but it took about four hours. Then finally, we were here, right on the border to freedom. All we had to do was wade across a small stream and walk about one mile, and we would be free at last! Phil, we will have to take off our shoes and roll up our trousers.

'Mr Sean, do you have any tissue, I have to go behind a bush, you know what I am saying?'

'Yeah sure, Phil, be quick.' 'Will do Mr Sean'

'Ahhhh, are you ok, Phil?'

Phil came hopping out with his trousers at his ankles. 'No, shit, I have been bitten by a snake.'

'What colour is the snake?' Adentric asks with a worried look on his face.

'Red and pink, red and pink, Adentric.' Phil almost screams.

'Oh my god Phil, those snakes are the most venomous snakes in the world. Phil, painful death would follow if the poison not sucked out in fifteen minutes.'

'Mmmrr Seann, what is going to happen?' 'Phil, you are going to die because I am not going to suck out the poison out of your ass mate, so make your peace with God.'

'Mr Sean, you cannot do that to me, we go back years and years.'

'Hahaha, we got you there, Phil, it was only a ground snake; your ass will nip for a couple of hours, mate, that is all.'

'The pair of you are fecking bastards; you had me thinking I was going to die out here in Columbia.

However, Phil look at your left arm mate, it is gushing with blood, did you fall? Rip off a piece of the tee-shirt to make a bandage, and I will tie it as best as I can till we get across the border because it is going to have to be stitched up ASAP mate. How's that, is it not too tight?'

No, that is good, Mr Sean, but the bandage is thick with blood; we have to get a move on mate.'

'Mr Sean, Phil, I cannot let you cross the border.' Adentric said, pointing a gun at the both of us.

'You have sold the both of us out, you dirty Columbian bastard, 'Et tu' Adentric, I see you understand Latin Mr Sean, 'Thank you Mr Sean for your kind words; hand it over now, while I was it the fuel station, it was on the news that Pablo Escobar has put a price on your head for $150,000,000, give it to me now, what Pablo wants so bad that he is going to pay $150,000,000.

Nikki, who has been quiet until now, suddenly looks at myself and Phil. 'Just give it to the both of us, or the pair of you will be shot.' *So much for loyalty to Phil, bitch.*

'Adentric, Nikki, you will never shoot myself or Phil.'

'Feck sake Mr Sean, what are you saying, they have the gun pointed at the both of us.'

'Why is that Mr Sean?' 'Well, you do not have any fecking bullets for a start.'

'Why is that Mr Sean?' 'Well, when the both of you were in getting fuel, I checked under the passenger seat of your car because, Maria told me while I was in Pablo garage that a Columbia man always keeps his gun there, guess what? I took the bullets out, here they are.'

As I unclenched my left fist, six lovely silver bullets fell to the ground.

'Adentric, you want them, we fight for them, just you and me over there by the rock. If I win, we go free and if you win, I will give you the internet stick.'

'That is a deal, Mr Sean.'

'Phil, hold onto that Columbia bitch.'

'I forgot to tell you, Mr Sean, am a mix-martial arts fighter.'

Fuck, never saw that one coming, remember the saying in jail, kill or be killed, time to rumble.

'Adentric, I too have studied the act of martial art called dim-mak, (*it means death point striking, the deadliest pressure point on the body is the easiest to get to, stomach point number 9 located, level with the tip of Adam's apple, just on course of the carotid artery, on the anterior border of the sternocleidomastoids muscle, half an inch from Adam's apple, it is one of the major dim-mak death points on the body*) look it up dim-mak.'

A light strike will cause a knockout and a hard blow over this point will cause death; now am not saying that am Mr Miyagi of the dim-mak world but do not try out these pressure points without learning about them first, because one day, they will save your life or your loved ones.

He hits me with about four (4) rapped punches, (*feck he is good*), as Adentric throws his fifth punch, I parry it to the left, thus opening up at 9, X marks the spot, shit missed it. He then roundhouse kicks me to the left side of my head, down I go. He dives on me ready to unleash a flurry of punches. To the left of my head, there was a fist-sized stone, I grabbed it and smashed it off the side of his jaw and stomach, 5 points, another 'KO' pressure point, the job finished, he will not get up from that, *I had to re-establish my breathing pattern*, he was good Phil.

'Nice move Mr Sean, remember Phil, there is only one rule in street fighting.'

'And that is Mr Sean?' 'There is no rule,

'Strike first,

strike hard,

no mercy.'

'Phil, there is a reason that man never had a suntan, it is because he always walks in the shade. Take off their shoelaces, and tie the both of them up, and let us get the hell out of Columbia. My *mouth was dry as Myself and Phil stared up into the night sky, frozen looking at the cloud of flying vampires blocking out the moonlight, Pablo knows we have escaped Phil, and he knows we are heading out of Colombia, and the werewolves will not be far behind.'*

Yes, I know Mr Sean.'

It's 20 minutes before sunrise, we must keep on moving Phil, for our good and wellbeing we cannot let these Aliens find the pair of us now Phil.

Phil looks at Nikki, who looked both scared and worried. 'He will be ok, Nikki, he is just knocked out.'

'Please take me with you, I will be killed if I stay here.' 'Sorry, we cannot trust you, what will be will be. Goodbye forever.'

As Phil blew her a kiss, we waded across the stream.

'Phil, I am going to go back across the stream, and give Nikki my bank card.'

'Why are you doing that, Mr Sean? she was going to hand the both of us over to that cunt Pablo.'

'Phil, if it were not for her, we would still be in jail.'

'Remember blood is thicker than water, it was her brother Adentric that put her up to this.'

'I guess you are right, Mr Sean, remember to pick up the haversack.'

Good thinking Phil, I had all most forgot about the haversack.

'Nikki!' *I screamed her name.* 'Mr Sean, have you come back to take me with you?' 'No, here is my bank card, there is $200,000 in it, look after yourself, goodbye. As I walked away, I turned around and looked her in the eyes, and *kicked her in the pussy.*

Phil we will have to walk the rest of the way not on the trail, but in the jungle for camouflage, but first, let us cover our scent with this pepper. As *I scattered the pepper all over the jungle floor.* Meanwhile, we can hear the werewolves, running through the jungle like a fleet of bulldozers, smashing their way through the Amazon rainforest. Knocking down trees and breaking them like they were cocktail sticks. They were some distance away. We are not going to outrun these Ancient Aliens, it is 20 minutes to go until sunrise, now they are 100 meters from myself and Phil, and closing fast.'

Phil, hurry up, or they will be on top of the pair of us mate.'

It is no good, Mr Sean, cannot go any faster, I am losing too much blood, and I do not want to bleed out.

We can smell the breath of these werewolves being carried by the Colombian night air. All of a Sudden we stopped frozen, there in front of the pair of us was about 15 werewolves, all standing upright, saliva dripping from their mouths like a pack of wolves with rabies. Mr Sean, Phil nice to meet the pair of you again, it was Blackie and the rest of Pablo's sicarios. Blackie? you can talk while you have transformed into the Alien *werewolves*'

'Yes we can now please hand over the information you have stolen from Pablo, the both of you are going to die, but if you hand it over it will be a quick kill, you have my word. We will not rip your body to pieces, as the pack of werewolves moved in for the kill.

Here take it, as I threw the memory stick, it landing a few feet away from the pack of *werewolves* as they walk past the memory stick, we are going to rip yourself and Phil, to pieces now.

As Phil turned to me, and said, let them kill me first Mr Sean and he pushed me to the back of him. The werewolves were getting closer, saliva dripping from their fangs. They were about two meters away, they were sniffing the air, it was like smelling something that they did not like, blood was now running down Phil's arm on to the ground, as Phil and I said spontaneously *"It's always the darkest just before the dawn"*

as we walk through the valley of the shadow of death, I fear no evil, God does not walk with me he carries me, man, god bless the martyrs. Mr Sean, Phil you cannot run with the big dogs if you pee like a puppy. Then it happened, the lead werewolf pounced at Phil, *this is where everything goes in to slow motion,* going in *for the kill,* Phil screamed in terror, lifting his left arm in a futile way to block the attack, causing the blood to splatter over the werewolf face, all of a sudden Blackie, the main werewolf howled in agonizing pain and vaporized, ' I shouted at Phil it is your blood that kills these mother fuckers. Phil ripped off his blood-soaked Man-made bandage, swirling it frantically above his head as the other werewolves came in for the kill, little specks of Phil's AB-negative blood, hitting and vaporizing them. Pablo's bloodthirsty werewolves who were his top sicarios, were all vaporized into the Colombian morning air. You did it, Phil you fucking did it! Man you took out all of the fucking werewolves, you're a legend Phil, a total legend mate. You saved both of us, you did it, man you did it, I have never been so scared in all my life Phil. It is your rare blood group that kills these werewolves.'

What type of blood is it you have, Phil? Phil are you ok? He stood like a marble statue frozen in time, Phil speak to me mate. As he came round, he said, Mr Sean I think I am going to have to change my boxershorts cause I have shit myself mate. Laughing and looking into Phil's eyes, dinnae worry about it mate so have I. As we stood there coming to terms with what has just happened. That is the first time and hopefully the last time a fecking werewolf talks to me Mr Sean. As *the sun broke over the treetops, its rays killing off the Colombian darkness,* Mr Sean remember to pick up the memory stick.' I sure will Phil, and look there's a sign on the road up ahead it reads, Welcome to Venezuela. We made it Phil we fucking did it man, and we do not have to worry about those fecking *werewolves and vampires* because they cannot change in the day time.'

It is a great feeling Mr Sean, and it will not be long before we are homeward bound. It has been an incredible journey. I'm going to have to try and stitch this wound up; we have not got the time to go to a hospital. I have only lost about half a pint of blood, I will survive. After what we have just happened I will survive anything, big boy. Still, I have a sense that that will not be the last time we encounter these, *"murder puppies and bloodsuckers."*

I know Phil, and it has been a total nightmare mate, but let us keep the celebrations on ice until our feet are back in Dundee.

Meanwhile, 300,000 soldiers, police, plus *werewolves and vampires* were looking all over Colombia for Phil and me, and we were in good old Venezuela. All we have to do is walk three (3) miles into the city of San Cristobal and hire a taxi to Caracas, then meet up with Tony and go to the airport. Within 48 hours, we will be back home in Dundee, Scotland.

We hailed a taxi on the road which stopped to pick up Phil and I. 'Spero's hotel, Catacus.'

As the taxi driver drove to Caracas, we just sat in silence, looking out of the window, thinking about everything that we had been through in the last four months since we landed in Columbia.

, When you said to Adentric 'Et tu'and, he said I hear you understand Latin,

Well, what does 'Et tu' mean?

An unsuspected betrayal by a friend, mate.

You're right there mate, and I never even made out with his sister, and here was me thinking we were going to spend the rest of our lives together, mate.

Well, mate, I think you have had enough of Colombian girls, but she was perfect looking mate.

'Taxi driver, can you tell me the final football score with Germany and Japan?'

'Germany 3 Japan 6.' 'So, it will be Columbia v Japan in the world-cup-final.' 'Yes, and my name is Jack Murdoch and not, taxi driver.'

'Sorry, we never introduced ourselves, my name is Santiago, and my friend is called Mateo, Jack is an unusual name for a man in Venezuela.'

'Yes, it is, I was named after the great Scottish physicist doctor jack Murdoch, my father worked with doctor jack Murdoch at the NASA space centre.'

'Cool, was your father working on the I. O. N. propulsion for space travel when Doctor Jack discovered it?'

'No, unfortunately, my father had left NASA for a job with the Columbian government at the time, but my father and doctor jack remain good friends to this day.'

'Santiago, do you know the physicist doctor jack?'

'No, but I do know of him, he was born in a Scottish village called Blairgowrie. I know this because I once worked in the Scottish city of Dundee, it is about 14 miles away from where he came from.'

'It is amazing the people a person can meet at the back of a taxi. I know you are wondering why my father is so clever and rich and why I am working as a taxi driver?'

'Well, it did cross my mind, Jack.' 'I am in my final year of neurosurgery residency, my final 7th year. Gentlemen, we will soon be at the Spero hotel, it has been a pleasure meeting the pair of you.'

'Likewise, jack.' 'Enjoy your stay.' 'Thank you here is $100, keep the change.'

As we walk along the path to the hotel. 'Here, Mr Sean, why did you tell the taxi driver different names.' 'Phil, you never know, Pablo has people everywhere, and no doubt, people in authority in the Americas will be looking for two Scottish guys with British passports.'

'That is why we will be traveling with fake German passports.'

'Mr Sean, you sure plan everything down to the last detail.'
'Better to be safe than sorry, Phil.'

'I will give Tone a call to tell him we are here. Hello Tone it is me, Sean and Phil, we are outside the hotel, come down and meet the both of us.'

'Sean, where are the rest of you, it is a long story, just come down, and I will tell you everything about it.'

***

'Hey bro, free at last, and you are looking well Phil too. It has been a fucking nightmare in that shit-hole of a prison but now, the both of you are out, come up to my room, and let us get out of this place, the pair of you will be looking forward to getting home. Here, put on these German football shirts.'

'Germany got a beating by Japan in the semi's.' 'Yes, we know, the taxi driver told me, there will be thousands of German fans flying home tonight.'

'Here are the passports, your name Sean, is Hans Mercedes and Phil, your name is Adimaro Muller, and here are your tickets.' Tone said, *sounding happy.*

We need to get a tube of superglue to seal up Phil's arm wound just in case, hope the cabin pressure does not make it start bleeding again.

We just surreptitiously slipped through the customs, as we were taxiing down the runway, I think we all had a lump in our throats.

After five minutes have passed, we finally lift off out of the nightmare.

We arrived back home in Dundee, Scotland, 22 hours after we had left Venezuela and 41 hours after we had left el-shithole jail in Columbia.

At the arrival hall, everybody was there, all our family and friends, ever notch was there,tail wagging as always, well half a tail, as his tail was cut short when he was a puppy.

It was a very emotional reunion, but we had done it. We pulled a "Keyser Soze" on Columbia and Pablo Escobar. The world's richest man. But most of all, we had all the information on the internet stick to bring down the world's first multi-trillionaire and the evilest drug baron in the world.

'Here, Phil, looks at this fecking beauty, as I showed Phil the other ring.'

'That is my ring Mr Sean, how did you get that?'

'I took it from Rahul's finger, remember when I said I had to go back to the cell for my phone, well that is when it went into the room where all the guards were, tripping out their heads and I took it from Rahul, his head was so much up his arse, he never knew what was going on and Phil, it is our ring because I had to sell my own to get the pair of us out of jail and Columbia.'

'Yeah sure, Mr Sean, that is cool with me big boy.'

Everybody knew our story. There were TV cameras with reporters trying to get an interview with myself, and Phil. A top newspaper offered a large sum of money for the first interview. It was all too much, we had to tell everybody that we would not be saying anything to anybody.

In the last four days, we had much catching up to do with family and friends, and I cannot believe we made it back home. I am looking forward to spending my first night in my bed, I have wished for this moment since we were set up and put in jail by that bastard, Pablo Escobar.

Two days later, we were still getting hounded by newspapers, reporters, and tv crews. *I am going to phone Phil and see how he is doing.* 'Hey Phil.' 'Mr Sean, isn't it fucking great been out of that shit hole of jail and Columbia.' 'You took the words right out of my mouth, Phil.'

'Mr Sean, I was catching up with some newspapers, and the Columbian Government grounded all the planes that were going to the UK from taking off; and they ordered all the planes that were flying to the UK to return to the airport in the Americas or the Columbian Airforce would shoot them down.'

'Phil, I knew that cunt Pablo Escobar would do that once he found out we had escaped with all the information we had about his Olmec cartel and the drug routes for his cocaine trafficking.'

'That is why I got German passports made because no way would he be thinking we will be flying to Germany. Pablo likes to be 13 steps ahead of everybody. All I needed is to be one step ahead of him, and Phil; I am going to phone the American embassy in Edinburgh.'

'Why are you going to do that, Mr Sean?'

'Well, I am going to give them all the info that we have on Pablo Escobar, and they will pass it onto the president of America. He will, in turn, be in the position with w.d.a.a.d. to start to dismantle Pablo's drug empire because President Trumpet hates Pablo Escobar; he is always using disparaging remarks about him, and likewise with Pablo.'

'Cool, Mr Sean, tell me how you get on.' 'Sure will Phil.' 'Ok, cheers, big boy.'

TWO HOURS LATER

Come on, Phil, pick up the phone.

'Hello Phil, Mr Sean here, I have spoken to the American ambassador to Scotland, and he was very interested in the information, he is going for a summit in Copenhagen, and he will be back on Tuesday; and has arranged a meeting with the both of us for Friday the13th next week. That cunt Pablo fecking Escobar will never forget this Friday the 13th in a long time.'

'Oh, Mr Sean, I have just agreed that both of us will appear on a breakfast Tv show in Glasgow. To tell the truth, Mr Sean, I do not want to appear on Tv.'

'That is no problem, Phil, I will go down to Glasgow, and you can go to the American embassy with the internet stick, he knows all about our story as he has been following it on the news, it is a Mr Carrie, you have to ask for.

'Cool, no problemo Mr Sean.'

FRIDAY THE 13TH

In the car with Phil, I was thinking to myself. 'Today is the date we sink Pablo Escobar's drug empire, right Phil? I will drop you off at the American Embassy in Edinburgh, and I will drive to Glasgow for the interview. I also have a meeting with a reporter, from *Republican* Mr Frank Stagg, then I will come back and hopefully meet the ambassador, but go in and show him all the information we have on Pablo. I will catch up with you later on, say in about two hours. Phil, that national newspaper has put on a welcome home party for us on Saturday, they are just running our story to sell their paper. There will be many reporters at this party, remember, do not say anything about the information we have on Pablo

Escobar's drug empire, and do not say anything about the *werewolves and vampires.*

'Yes, I know Mr Sean not to say anything, and the other prominent newspapers are running a campaign to get me and you extradited to Columbia, just because we never agreed to tell them our story.

'Phil that is life mate. For every person that welcomes us home, there will be another two people that will see us as drug smugglers. Nevertheless, I do not give a fuck what anybody thinks anymore, fuck the lot of them, they are just pot-lickers.'

Regardless, Phil, I will catch up with you later on, mate ok, after you have been to the American embassy and remember Phil the world-cup-final is being played on Sunday, "Columbia v Japan," we can go out and watch it and have a few drinks.'

'That is fine with me, Mr Sean.' 'Here, Mr Sean, I'd like to thank you a lot, mate.' 'Thank me for what Phil?'

'Just for everything, mate, if it were not for you, I do not think I would have made it out of that place alive.' 'Yeah, well, Phil, you help me a lot too mate.'

'Really Mr Sean, you seemed relaxed all of the time.' 'only because you were with me Phil and I knew we would get out of that place together Phil. We will be mates till the end of time, and then a day after that, but remember one thing, Phil.'

'And what would that be, Mr Sean?'

'no pussy is worth fifty-five (55) fecking years in jail, mate, we will be at the embassy in a few minutes, Phil.'

'Here, Mr Sean, I forgot to ask something?' 'Yeah, Phil, fire away.'

'Remember the lawyer in Colombia, Marco Gomez?'

'Yeah, course I do' 'You were telling him about when you walked into the room, and two men were snorting cocaine off a young girl's body.'

'Are you going to get on with it Phil, we are almost at the embassy!'

'Ok, Mr Sean, settle down, you said there were two more men in the corner giving two girls a "Columbian snowstorm'

'Yes, I remember.'

'Well, Mr Sean, are you going to tell me, what is a "Columbian snowstorm"?'

'For fuck sake Phil, we have been in one of the worst jail in the world, and we have seen people getting murdered at least five times a day over the past months. We have heard people screaming in agony while they are getting tortured by Rahul and his prison guards. I am surprised that cunt Rahul can sit down with their feet sticking out of his ass because prisoners are shit scared of him, and not to mention the *werewolves and vampires;* the only thing that's been bothering you is a fucking "Colombian snowstorm"!'

'Yeah, it is just something I have been thinking about, are you going to tell me?

'Well Phil, a "Columbian snowstorm" is when a man puts cocaine up his asshole and farts, and the female or male snorts the cocaine in the air like a Columbian snowstorm, are you happy now Phil?'

'That is the most disgusting thing I have ever heard about, who tae fuck thinks up these acts of grossness?'

'Well, Phil, you know what they say.'

'What is that Mr Sean?'

'do not knock it till you have tried it.' 'I think I will give that Miss Mr Sean.'

'Hahaha.'

Remember, when I ask you what cartoon character you would like to be?

Phil, you remember some crazy stuff mate, yes, I do why?

Well, are you going to tell me!

I want to be Bugs Bunny, because he, like myself never gets caught, like Yosemite Sam, and Elmer Fudd, they are always trying to catch Bugs.'

'And one more question Mr Sean are you going to tell me what you said to Jennifer to get her to dance with you at the smoo party, after party?'

'Yes, sure, mate, I will tell you after I pick you up at the embassy. What is that you have in your hand, Phil?

It is a small knife I use for cleaning my fingernails.

Phil put that way do not be cleaning your nails out in my dad's car, I am not here to clean up after you mate.'

'cool, Mr Sean, see you then, big boy.' 'Here, Phil, I was thinking last night, Dundee is fecking beautiful man!'

'You do not appreciate something until you lose it.' Phil said, nodding his head.

'I took notch for a walk up to the woods at 6 am, just walking through the woods, peace, and quiet, and to see all the wildlife. You know Phil, it was great, money cannot buy that, no money in the world can buy that!'

'You have knocked that right on the head there, Mr Sean, Dundee is the best place in the world.'

'Well, it is better than that shite hole of jail in Columbia, and we will never have to see that bastard, Pablo Escobar.

"Pablo Escobar and the Olmec cartel you are terminated"

Remember Phil, even the Star ship Enterprise had a self-destruct button, and you sure did press your own, nobody messes with the cartels and walks away from them.

The embassy is very palatial, with its marble floors and winding stairways, but you first need to go through the security checks, and that was before entering the main building.

'Hello.' I said to the female at the main desk. 'Mr Sean, here to see Ambassador Carrie.'

'one moment Mr Sean, I will notify Ambassador Carrie that you are here as she clicked on their intercom.'

'Mr Sean, Ambassador Carrie, will be right down.'

'Thank you.'

'Mr Sean, I am Ambassador Carrie, please follow me into my office.' we shake hands smiling.' 'Take a seat, would you like some tea or coffee, Mr Sean?'

'Coffee please, milk, no sugar. *As I am sweet enough.*

Ambassador Carrie was like a typical Texan. He wore a ten-gallon hat, snakeskin cowboy boots, and had the whitest teeth I have ever seen on anybody, let alone a man.

'I believe you have some important information about Pablo Escobar's Drug Empire, Mr Sean.'

'Yes, here, it is all on this internet stick. As Mr Carrie looked over the information, his eyes lit up. 'This information will be very crippling to the drug trade, not only in American but worldwide.

'I forgot to tell you, ambassador, I am not Mr Sean, he is away to Glasgow doing an interview I am Phil.' 'I see you are the person that was with Mr Sean in Columbia.'

'Yes ambassador, that six months was hell on earth.'

The next thing that occurred was the ambassador reaching for the red phone that was on his desk.

'It is not Mr Sean, but his friend, Phil.' He calmly spoke into the phone. 'Please, you may come in now.' He looks at me, smiling, putting down the phone.

The door bursts open, and in walks, Pablo Escobar and his sicario's.

No fucking way! We have been set up, that American ambassador is in Pablo's Escobar pocket.

'Ambassador, thank you for your good work; £ 150 million is being transferred to your Swiss bank account as we speak.' 'Thank you, Don Pablo.' 'You have been paid well for your good work.'

'Phil, nice to see you and thank you for bringing me the information that Mr Sean stole from Maria's computer. May I be so bold to ask, where is Mr Sean?'

'He is driving to Glasgow, Don Pablo.' 'Please phone him.'

'Hello, Mr Sean.'

'Hi, how are you doing, Phil? Did everything go well with the ambassador?

'Well, no.'

'come again, Phil?'

Pablo takes the phone away from Phil.

'Hello, Mr Sean, it is your old friend here, Pablo Escobar. I have come for the information that you stole from me back in Columbia. I have it now, and it is time for me to say my final farewell. Your Friend Phil is an escaped fugitive from Columbia and it is my duty to take Phil back to the prison he escaped from in Columbia. Mr Sean, the drug trade kills more people than war, please remember this, and for Phil's sake do not tell anyone about anything you have seen in Colombia. Goodbye.

'Wait, Don Pablo, you have the information, there is no need to take Phil back with you, let me say a last goodbye to Phil, Pablo.

I am coming to get you, Phil, *as I whispered to Phil, use the knife.*

'*Pablo suddenly snatches the phone from Phil*; how did you manage to kill my sicarios and the prison correctional officers? Mr Sean, luckily, I have had them all cloned. Pablo myself or Phil never did anything to your men, *shouting so Phil would hear me*. As I said before, Mr Sean, goodbye.'

** The End **

Or is it!

Copyright disclaimer

"Words and phrases from the Scottish dialect, translated into English below

I dinnae ken =I do not know

Ken what I mean =do you know what I am saying

Cannae=can't

Oot ya=out of you

Tae=too

Tattie pickers=potatoes pickers

Gee 'us=give me

Dinnae lose your Heid=don't lose you head

Eh'll hae twa peh's=I will have two pies

An ingin ane an eh=an onion in as well

Gie ya a skelpit lug=hit you in the ear with my hand

Haud your wheesht loon=please don't talk

We'll hay tae skedaddle aff=we will have to go now

F'it like loon is yer h'ands cald=how are you doing is your hands cold.

Bairns=children

Big Baz=Big balls.

Printed in Great Britain
by Amazon